MW00973759

Riddles for the Kingdom

By C. M. Bolte

Pen It! Publications

© 2017

ISBN #:   978-1542997089

ISBN #:   1542997089

Edited by: Wanda Williams

Cover Art and Illustrations by: Savannah Horton

First Edition © 2017

To Lindsay Best Wishes Cindy Bolte

Pen It! Publications, LLC
penitpublications@yahoo.com
www.BuyMeBooksNow.com
penitpublications@yahoo.com

Dedication

This book began as a family project when my children were learning how to write a story for school. One of my deepest desires was for my children to learn and appreciate stories in the written form and to interject the adventure and fun into the art of writing. From my children, ideas flowed; illustrations were sketched (although not used for this book). It became a fun collaboration which inspired the children to keep it going. Over time, the ideas were not lost, but the schedules prevented us from working on it together so much. I continued this great, fun adventure.

Occasionally one of the children would say, "How's the book coming?" As I would tell them, they would become engaged again, giving me more ideas, excited about 'our' project. I was so thrilled to be able to work with my children. While I hope that I taught them something, I have learned the wonderful freedom of imagination and fantasy. I shared our story, yet unfinished, with my brother and my mother. They encouraged me to finish.

So, as I have continued to travel through the land of Swindalia to see where our adventure would take us, the book became a part of me and I a part of it. I decided that whether it published or not, the experience with my children and the encouragement of my family would always be priceless.

Thank you Katie, Zachary and Jacob, my beloved

Pen It! Publications, LLC

children. What a fun creation and a privilege to have worked on this with you. Thank you, Mom, now 88 years old, who always inspires and dreams big, and thank you Dave, who 'gets' me and pushed me to get it done. Finally, thanks be to my Creator who has instilled in me the desire to write and the talent to do so. Without Him, no words would have been written.

To all of the children and parents who can connect by doing a project like this, I dedicate this book. The saying goes, "time flies, and you can't get that time back." Embrace the precious time with your children and allow your 'inner child' to come out to play, making memories that will last forever.

Preface

Consider for a moment experiencing life that takes place long ago....a time before our modern world of chaos....before cars, before trains or planes, before cowboys and Indians. The lifestyle of this time, if you can imagine, was very different.

This was a time of Knights and dragons, Kings and Queens, where nothing seemed impossible, and where nothing was as it seemed, except for the ominous emerging spiritual conflict between good and evil.

Pen It! Publications, LLC

Introduction

Beginning a book by explaining the beauty and majesty of a land as blissful can be misleading, because without conflict, there would be no story. This is true for this story.

The land seemed to be a beloved place where people lived happily in a community filled with farmers, townspeople and businessmen who worked together for the good of all. There was, seemingly, peace throughout the land. However, unbeknownst to them, an evil that had slithered into this land, held at bay for so long, was beginning to rumble and reemerge.

Chapter 1

$\mathscr{T}$he people were content farming their lands or working their trade. There was the local merchant, Mr. Flandenburg, who owned and operated the local Flandenburg's Trading Post. He seemed to never know a stranger, even when one did come into his shop. He not only was the store manager, but the pharmacist for the people, as well.

Mr. Flandenburg always had a cure for what ailed a person. But his favorite thing to do, was to watch the children come into the store. He always had a sugary treat, just for them. Their eyes would brighten just coming in the door, because they knew that Mr. Flandenburg would surprise them with something special. Everyone loved Mr. Flandenburg for his kindness and generosity. But this was not a rare quality of people living in this place.

Mr. Macaroy, the local blacksmith, took care of all the horses and wagons in the community and served as animal doctor for the farmer's livestock. Twice a week he traveled to the Palace to tend to the King's horses and always took a treat for the kittens. When they saw him, they would attack him in the barn with meows and purrs. Mr. Macaroy had a way with animals, all of them. It was as if he could talk to them.

He understood them and they, likewise, understood him.

The farmers had a rich and giving soil, making them always prosper in their harvest. The kingdom was located on the outer region of a land, not known to us now. Little is known today of this beautiful land as it has come to pass; like the honor and bravery of knights fighting the mighty dragons of old. It was a time of mystical things. There were flowing rivers of fresh, cool water, rolling hills, green pastures, and white capped mountains in the distance, all which surrounded the castle where their King lived. Seasons would change from winter into spring and then summer into fall. It was always beautiful to behold.

This was the Kingdom known as Duradane. The people of this region were kind to one another. And while the land was governed by a King, its village people were permitted to enter the realms of the kingdom and welcomed as important guests. This was a time of great majesty, adventure and hope that life was good in the eyes of Duradane's people.

King Theyman ruled with love for his people and his land. He treasured its beauty. The King was middle-aged and, while his hair was graying from what was once handsome black, he was full of life and wise in his aging years. His beard and mustache were also graying to a salt and peppery look, but they were well kept and cut close to his face. People would often comment how wonderfully childlike he was. But his youth-like demeanor did not distract him from the seriousness of his responsibilities as King.

King Theyman loved his horses and enjoyed the pleasure of their company. It was not uncommon for the villagers to see their King riding his beautiful white stallion throughout the countryside. Some would say it was for pleasure, but truly it was to oversee his people.

He would normally be seen wearing his crown, adorned with a single red ruby embedded in the front of it. This crown had been handed down from many generations. Since its origination, the stone, from time to time, had to be reset. The value was not in the stone, but in its meaning. It represented a long line of gracious Kings.

King Theymen's father had taught his son not only how to be a King, but how to be a good man, a kind man, a strong man.....and a good father to his own son.

As he rode on his great steed, his shoulders would be draped with a dark green, velvet robe with a jade pendant used to grasp its sides around his neck. His boots were black leather, shiny and tall, fitting snug on his forelegs, running up to just below the knee. He also carried his sword that draped down his side from his slender waist. This was more for show than for use as a weapon. He was never flashy or arrogant, but distinctively royal.

On occasion he would stop at a villager's home for a cup of tea and a visit. He smelled of tobacco, for if there was one bad habit that the King enjoyed, it was the pleasure of smoking his pipe. The sweet smell of the peppermint tobacco lingered in the air, about him and on his clothes.

The King adored and cherished his wife, Queen Maritta. They had been married for 35 years and he would commonly tell people that he loved her more today than the day they were wed, all those many years ago. She dressed simply and delicately. Her features were attractively feminine. One might see her in the villages mingling with the people at the market. She, of course, did not have to do this, having so many attendants, but she loved her people, as did their King. She, too, was mild mannered, but she was set apart by her beauty and grace. Her dress was normally long and flowing, made of silk and cotton with a petite string of lace to adorn just the sleeves and the neckline.

Queen Maritta would wear her tiara upon her head of long golden hair, a perfect accent to her beautiful face. King Theyman would often tell her that her hair looked like spun gold; with her, he would always be a rich man. While she was getting older, like her husband, there was always beauty, youth, and vitality in her deep brown eyes.

Every year, King Theyman would celebrate his land and his people with a large festival. There were games, feasts, music, magicians and royal court jesters, fireworks, fun, laughter, storytelling, and singing....oh the SINGING! The people loved to sing loud, long, and happily. During this time of celebration, they could be heard singing for hours at a time. This festival had been the tradition of this land for hundreds of years.

Their stories were tales passed down through the generations of dragons and wizards, elves, and other unusual creatures. Of course, no one had seen these things. Competitions would be held to see who could tell the best story. Young children and even adults would allow themselves the adventure of imagining and dreaming of the creatures still roaming this land.

However, there were rumblings of unseen evil waiting for just the right time to show itself. It was during one such festival, that this peaceful dwelling was to be challenged.

It was the autumn of the year during the celebration of the harvest. The evening was late, the music was loud, great fireworks were exploding into the night sky....reds, blues, golds, yellows and greens; every color of the rainbow, vibrant variations in hues. Truly, it was a site to behold. The oohs and ahhhh's with each celebration seemed to echo the belief that this year's light show was better than the last.

King Theyman, having enjoyed the celebrations, had decided to retire for the evening. His wife, the Queen, had been escorted back to the castle several hours earlier. The path to the inside of his castle was long, steep and dark, but being loved by all and unafraid to walk home unaccompanied, he announced his good night and started on his way. As he began to walk, the noise of the festival was fading; the darkness grew more pronounced and the quiet to a deafening silence. The lights on the path were foot candles that had been lit by his grounds men earlier in the evening.

Beads of sweat were breaking out to his brow. *Had he had too much wine this evening?* He walked faster then stopped, considering his surroundings, and looked around, seeing nothing in the vastness of the dark. He began to walk again...faster...faster. He was becoming breathless, his chest heaving, partly from fear and partly from the quick long strides of his pace.

"What is wrong with me?" he thought to himself, unaware of having ever known panic like this before... *"And why am I so uneasy?"* His thoughts were racing. Fear now dominated him... sweating... thinking only of his destination... when suddenly....he stopped. The sound of his heart beating was so loud he knew that it would be heard by anyone listening, giving his presence away.

The path lights were gone. *When had they been blown out? Had the wind been blowing?* Funny that he would not have noticed the wind. He looked to the side of the path and there on the ground lay his wife's maiden and the two knights who had been accompanying her.

Thoughts of panic began to run through him. *Where was Queen Marietta? Was she safe? Had someone taken her?*

Pen It! Publications, LLC

Chapter 2

*O*ver the next several months, efforts to find the King and Queen had been unsuccessful. Shortly after his disappearance, the Duradane Kingdom was attacked. From a foreign land came the Seltons, a nation known for their terror and destruction. Though the King's leadership had kept these ruthless scavengers at bay for many years, without his leadership, the Seltons had no fear. They were emboldened to challenge the people of Duradane. They came from beyond the mountain ranges, burning and destroying the beauty of the land, taking over the kingdom.

Darkness began to cover the land. Its people became poor, as did the land itself, from neglect and abuse. Forests and trees were burned; the waters, once so fresh and clean, were now polluted by the spoils of war. Many were slain 'in the name of the Seltons'. All was thought forever lost.

King Theyman had disappeared, believed to have been captured and killed. His Queen had been found, however, she was locked in the tower's pinnacle, guarded with no hope of freedom. The Kingdom was taken over by the leader of the Seltons. Duradane had never known evil such as this.

The leader of the Seltons was a Wizard. He was referred to as Froc and had used his powers to bestow a spell upon the Duradane's land. As the Seltons took over more and more of the land and villages, Froc began to rule the palace of Duradane.

But there was in this time, unknown to these Seltons, a prince, son of King Theyman. In an effort to preserve the Kingdom, and with hopes of one day conquering its attackers, the Knights of Duradane had taken Prince Darian to a safe place in the retreat of the forest. There he disguised himself and fought as one of the Knights of Duradane. He sought his father in earnest, his love never waning. His hope would not permit him to desert his King, his Father.

Chapter 3

*D*uradane's village people lived in fear for their lives. There were stories about the land of raids occurring on homes every day. No one was permitted to come into the castle or address the "Lord" of the castle. He was an evil ruler, just as he was an evil wizard. He took whatever he wanted from the people leaving them poor, hungry, and in despair.

One night in the village of Blue Haven, two children, Jemma and her brother, Frederick, had gone to bed. Their mother and father, just as they did every night, had come in and tucked them into bed, said their prayers together, and wished them a good night.

"Papa, will we ever get to go to the palace like you did when you were younger? I want to be a Knight!" said Frederick, the younger of the two children. Frederick was always full of questions, swinging his arms around like he had a sword and was fighting an evil dragon.

Papa smiled at him, remembering the peace of an earlier time, when swords were not needed and visits to the palace were welcomed. "Never lose hope, my boy...never lose hope. Now go to sleep! Both of you!" As Papa and Mama left the loft, there was one more "Good Night!" before all that the children could hear was a soft murmuring of their parents talking in the kitchen of their tiny home.

It was comforting listening to the quiet murmur of their parent's voices. There would be an occasional giggle from Mama or Papa, an apparent display of their love for each other. In the children's sleep, they were at peace dreaming of happier times, of laughter and of their land restored to a safe place. Even at their young ages, they realized that this place had become evil. But they felt protected in the confines of their home, under the protection of their father.

Suddenly they were awakened by the sound of men pounding on their house. As guardsmen pushed through the door, into the house, the children watched in silence, hidden in their loft, as their father tried to defend his home. The two children sat, watching and listening to their mother pleading for their lives. The guardsmen were unaware of the two children's presence. No mercy was given and their parents, with hands bound, were taken.

Would they be killed? Terror filled the night. The house began to burn. The children could smell the smoke, as it was filling the open spaces of their home. Heat was rising, as the fire began to engulf the house surrounding them. Jemma and Frederick, frozen in fear, knew that they had to get out!

"Quickly, Frederick, shhh! We must be very still, but we have to get out!" insisted Jemma.

Without another word and without grabbing more than their clothes, they slipped out of the bedroom window, falling to the hard ground and began running, arm in arm...running...one of them, then the other, tripping while one, then the other, kept the pace going as fast as they could... running... running... gasping for breath...running...no time to rest, their hearts pounding hard enough to explode from their chests...running...running...as fast as their young legs could carry them. Jemma tripped and fell to the ground.

"Hurry Jem! Get up! We have to hurry!" demanded Frederick as he pushed her to her feet.

"Where will we go?" cried the young girl. "Where would they have taken Mama and Papa?" Jemma erupted, not only falling to the ground again, but falling apart in fear. "We need to find Mama and Papa! We need to find them and help them!"

Even though Frederick was the younger of the two, his father had taught him how to take care of others in difficult situations. Right now, he was too scared to stop or to panic.

"Listen, Jemm, get a hold of yourself," Frederick said, as he pulled her back up to her feet again. "I don't know exactly where we need to go to be safe. All I know is that we must get away, as far as possible. We dare not follow them with the Seltons. We need to get some help. Now come on!"

The children began to run again. They ran deeper and deeper into the still misty woods. It was so dark and cold. They continued to run, as the mist thickened around them. They ran, too afraid to stop, or to cry, or even to mourn their parents. Suddenly they were abruptly stopped, as they both ran into something hard and tall. Bouncing off the object in their path, they both fell back onto the ground, stunned by the suddenness of the collision. Frightened, the children clung close to each other in hopes of protecting themselves, for just one moment more.

Pen It! Publications, LLC

Chapter 4

*J*emma and Frederick looked up and saw a kind face, worn and tired, but in his eyes there was a softness and concern. This face was framed by the open-faced plate of a knight's helmet, his breastplate engraved with the Duradane Crest. The children had run directly into a Knight! But, this was not just any knight.

As the stranger removed his helmet he said, "Don't be afraid. My name is Prince Darian, a noble Knight of my father's kingdom. I have been hiding in this forest and fighting alongside my fellow Knights to protect what we could of our land. Are you alright? What happened? Where have you come from?"

Trembling, but being the eldest, Jemma spoke, still breathless from running, "Our home has been attacked by the Seltons. They have taken our parents and burned our home. My brother and I have just barely escaped and we have been forced to run for our lives. We don't know where we are going. Where are we? Can you help us?"

"I can help you, yes, of course," began Prince Darian, in a gentle voice. "I will take you where you will be safe and cared for. We have an encampment on the other side of the ridge. You see? Up there," the Prince said, looking up and beyond the woods that now engulfed them.

It was difficult seeing anything just now with the thickness of the forest fog. The mist was beginning to clear and above them they began to see the twinkling of the stars, peaceful and safe, just as it had been at their home, not so long ago. It was odd that one could look up into the sky where nothing had changed. If the children could close their minds to the horror going on in this place and focus on the beauty of the stars, they might fool themselves into thinking they were safe. However, at this time and in this place, no one was safe.

--------------------<>--------------------

"Can you get up? Come now and hurry. Within these woods are spies for the evil wizard and his foot soldiers that roam through this area." The Prince said, as he stuck out his hands to help the two up from the wet, hard ground.

As they began to stand, a tree from behind Prince Darian began to move, twisting and turning, bending from its trunk, as if a living body were stretching from a long nap. It began to twist and reach for anything scrambling at its feet. This spell-ridden tree was ALIVE! It began to swing its large limbs, as though they were long, strong arms, sweeping from side to side trying to capture its prey. Bending, twisting and swinging, the giant of a tree caught the Prince. He began swinging him back and forth, and with a whip of its arms, he sent the young Knight into the air. He landed in a thicket, unconscious and injured.

No sooner had the assault began, it ceased and the monster once again reformed into the tree that it had been....tall, straight and still, but not until the Prince's body was broken. The children, standing stunned, broke loose from their frozen positions, having escaped once again from danger, and ran to his aid.

"Oh, Prince Darian, wake up! Are you okay?" cried Jemma. "He's not moving!"

"We have to hide him! We have to get some help!" exclaimed Frederick. "Jemma, you stay here with him and hide him the best that you can. I will go see if I can find help."

"No, Frederick! No!" cried Jemma.

"Look, Jemm," said Frederick, taking her by the arms and turning her to face him, "we have to get help. Sitting here idle only makes us more likely to get caught. You can do this. I won't be gone long. I know that the Prince told us the encampment was over the ridge, but it's too risky to go that far in the daylight. I'll just look close by. If he was out here on patrol, surely there will be others scattered about."

But the tricky part, Frederick knew, was to find the 'good guys' and not be found by any more Seltons....or weird, spell-bound trees.

By this time, the night was beginning to fade into morning and the first signs of the new day were emerging. Darkness was falling into the light on the horizon. Frederick slipped away, but returned shortly.

"There is a cave a short distance away, Jemma. We must get out of the daylight. We can take him to the cave and hide him during the daylight hours until we can get some help."

So the children began to drag the Prince, inch by inch, closer and closer to the cave. It seemed to take forever, but fear and the certainty of daylight approaching forced them to find both strength and speed. At last, they found the opening and their way into the deep mouth of the shelter. As they entered the small dark opening of the abyss, its walls began to collapse, rocks falling, sealing them in. Suddenly they found their situation had changed. They were trapped. There was no choice but to continue going forward, deepening their journey into this prison and hoping that there were no Seltons in here.

"There has to be a way out," they thought to themselves. *"Find the light; look for the light."*

Pen It! Publications, LLC

Chapter 5

*E*xhausted, Frederick and Jemma fell to the ground beside the Prince. Sleep swept over them as the overwhelming tiredness and ache of their bones possessed their weary bodies. Sweet sleep...a moment to dream of field's plush with flowers, of running freely in the pasture, of the scrumptious smell of Mama's lovely pies....

Awakened with a startle, Frederick sat straight up. "What was that?" he whispered.

Jemma groaned, as she slowly sat up, opening her eyes to the reality of their surroundings. They were indeed trapped in the cave and very much alone. A slight glimmer of light was sneaking in through the crevasses between the fallen rocks, allowing them to see a little better. Eyes adjusting, it was still very dark.

"Let's leave the Prince here. We can go find the way out and then come back to get him. We'll get some help," suggested the boy.

"That's what you said the last time...about getting help...See where that got us?" Jemma responded. "And what if something happens to him while we are gone? How will the kingdom ever be restored?" she asked, worried and confused about

Pen It! Publications, LLC

what they must do.

"Please Jemma," Frederick begged. "We cannot help him by staying here. If we are going to survive, we have to try!"

There was a sudden urgency to the reality of what they must do. They were now not just children, carefree and unburdened, but citizens of the Kingdom of Duradane. With that came a responsibility to their King and their people. Their youth was no longer an excuse to hide. A silent agreement was made between them, as they began to cover the Prince the best they could with leaves and branches that had collected and blown into the cave from years of abandonment. This would hopefully hide him from those that might somehow invade this place or someone that may try to dig the rocks away from the other side to get in.

As they began to creep further and further into the cave, both Jemma and Frederick gazed upon the light of a large golden object lying on the floor in front of them. As they approached, it became clear that it was an egg-like object. It was a large golden egg, rings of light radiated from around it. The closer the two got to the egg, they could hear a 'hum 'coming from it. At first, the sound was barely audible. However, as the light began to grow more pronounced, so, too, did the sound. The hum grew louder, more distinct, into a low voice then growing in volume, echoing throughout the spacious room. This was no ordinary voice. This was the voice of a wizard.

Before either could mouth a word, the voice

began to speak. It was like the light itself was talking, the light that continued to grow and materialize into a beautiful White Wizard. His magnificent glow filled the otherwise empty room with bright light. Both children in awe and in fear, held their breath, to not reveal their presence.

"I am the White Wizard, Jarrod." He spoke very slowly and deliberately. "I am here to protect the egg that lies before you. Why have you come here? What business brings you into this evil place?" the wizard inquired. "You do not look evil. Who sent you?"

Jemma spoke up, her frail, innocent voice barely audible, "We aren't evil. We are looking for help. Can you help us find a way out of here?" her voice trailed off into nothing.

The White Wizard did not miss a beat, nor did he seem to hear what Jemma had said. "Captured within the walls of this sphere is the dragon, Jade. The dragon is not just any dragon but the result of a curse from the Wizard Froc."

At the sound of this evil wizard's name, the children gasped. They knew that name and the horrible things that had happened since he had taken over the kingdom.

"Beware of this dragon, Jade. He is not a tame dragon."

Frederick leaned over and without hesitation said, "Is there any dragon that is tame? Papa told me there were no good dragons and---------"

"Shhh! Frederick! Be quiet!" demanded Jemma, as she was trying to listen to the White Wizard.

"...he has the power to take you to a land unknown to others, a place where evil dominates mystery and magic, a dark dominion. Anything can happen and probably the most unexpected of things will. To return from this place, you will need to find a locket and its key. This will unlock the passage to return to your land. Evil does not exist in this world without goodness somewhere. It would be up to you to find the allies needed for your success," warned Jarrod.

"Are you saying that the only way out of this cave is to go with this egg that is going to be a dragon, but hasn't even hatched yet? We need to find help now! Please! We cannot wait for this thing to hatch and grow up, not to mention the fact that you said that it wasn't friendly!" Frederick seemed to speak unapologetically.

"SILENCE!" exclaimed Jarrod.

The boy and the girl, shrank into smallness with fear.

"You must hear the rest of the story! Several hundred years ago, a Court Jester from the Kingdom of Duradane disappeared and has since never returned. It is presumed by the Wizarding order that this Jester had failed to find the locket. Why he was sent or where he disappeared is not known, although it is said that he fell into disfavor with the King. This Jester's name is Banion."

He hesitated, and then continued.

"When the dragon, Jade, wakens, hatching from the boundaries of the egg, his only desire will be to go to this land to obtain the locket and key. This will be his burning desire, at all costs. While he will not know why he has this immense need to get the locket and key, it will be his burning desire to retrieve them. Only through using the lock and key will his spell be broken. Bear in mind that the locket and key are not together, and there begins the challenge. In addition, the dragon, Jade, will not realize that he is the product of an evil spell, at first. We believe that this land, Swindalia, is filled with many dangers. Furthermore, we believe that the Court Jester still lives there with his dragon, Patarian. He is filled with hate and destruction for life itself. He is, you might say, MAD. His soldiers, you know as the Seltons."

The children were awe-struck with fright. Even Frederick, who loved when the elders and his own father would tell stories of the dragons of past, was horrified at what the Wizard was sharing.

"If you are called upon to go with Jade, you must go or face his wrath," warned Jarrod.

"Are you saying he will kill us?" asked Jemma, her voice trembling.

Ignoring her question, Jarrod continued, "Once there, at this land beyond, remember that your return is solely based on your success in finding the locket and key. You will not have much time. The continuum of time is different there. Exhausting your time will bear the consequence of never returning to your homeland. You would be lost forever. Beware!"

"How much time will we have?" Jemma asked urgently.

"That is one of the mysteries, I am afraid. No one knows, not even those of us in the Wizarding realm. Peace be with you."

As the sound of the White Wizard's voice echoed and began to fade into the cave, his light faded as well and the egg began to crack. The ground began to shake. Jemma and Frederick again clung to each other in fear. The crack in the outer shell widened and the children began hearing the sound of a creature screaming to be free.

Jemma and Frederick cried for help but the noise of the creature drowned out the sounds of their plea. Frightened and alone, they looked to find a place to run and hide. Behind them was a rock.

"There, Frederick! Behind the rock!" screamed Jemma, pulling her brother to safety.

As the egg opened, there emerged a great and powerful dragon, its wings opening into a magnificent creature. Its long, smooth neck, stretched to the confines of the ceiling. It had scales the color of polished jade. There was the smell of burning oil, sulfur, its breath was hot and fiery. The dragon's eyes widened, revealing a large darkened place behind them,

"I am the dragon, Jade, and much can be given

to those who seek my help. I have the power to heal and to save, if you but ask. But there is a price to pay for such power. Who is this that hides behind a rock? With my fire, I can destroy it and everything behind it! Again, I ask, who is this before me?!" roared the beast.

The children began to inch out from behind the rock, still cautious of this great creature.

"I am Frederick and this is my sister, Jemma. We are from the land of Duradane." Suddenly Frederick's mouth just wouldn't stop. "Wow! A real live dragon! You are just what I dreamt you would be like. We have run from our home. We are afraid of this evil that has taken over our land. "

As Frederick was finishing explaining to the creature about him and his sister, the dragon roared and blew a large blast of blue-orange flame over the heads of the small humans.

"Have MERCY! We mean you no harm. What do you want from us?" asked Frederick.

The dragon dropped his large head swinging it side to side, coughing and snorting, trying to clear his throat and his head. There was a sense of fear and confusion about him.

"You must go with me to the land of Swindalia where you must find a locket and key for me. I can only guess that my desire to possess these treasures is related to somehow unlocking the spell that has made me this vile creature. I have no memory of what I once was. I only know that I must return to what or who I was born to be."

Suddenly, the children felt a calmness wash over them. Was this another spell that had been put on them or truly was this creature kind, loving, sorrowful, one to be pitied, captured in this horrendous transformation?

"Did you say that you had the power to heal, Master Jade?" Asked Jemma.

The dragon's voice softened, "Yes, I do...why?"

"Our Pri... I mean our friend is injured..." said Jemma.

"No, Jemma! Don't say anymore!" advised Frederick.

"It's alright. I trust him," Jemma turned to address the dragon specifically. "Jade, our friend has been injured. Can you help him?" Jemma pleaded.

"Where is this friend? Take me to him."

With that, the children led Jade to the Prince and gently uncovered him so that his presence could be clearly seen. Still lying unconscious, the Prince did not move, his body lifeless and torn.

Jade moved closer to the body, studying him and noticing a familiarity about this small broken body. Great tears began to flow from his eyes falling upon the lifeless soul. Suddenly this body inhaled the deep, life-giving air from which he had been robbed. His breathing became long and even peaceful and restful.

"He will be well, but he will continue to be in a deep sleep until we return from our journey. Who is this 'friend'? He looks familiar."

The children looked at each other. *How could they trust him? How could they not? They must tell Jade the truth, or should they?*

"He is...um...a member of our village," the children said...stretching the truth.

Jade shook his head in contemplation, processing the information that the children had just shared with him. Then without further delay, Jade said, "Climb upon my back, both of you. We must go to the land of Swindalia.

"But how?" asked Jemma. "How do we get out of here?"

Jade once again showed his domination, roared and spewed his fire to the ceiling of this confined cavern. "Get on my back. We have no time to waste," Jade commanded.

Pen It! Publications, LLC

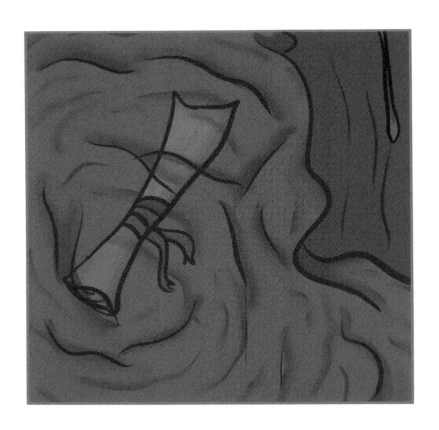

Chapter 6

There was no choice; the children had to go with Jade on this journey. Jade bowed down, so that the children could straddle this great monstrous beast. Jade rose and with a leap, he mounted the air above; his large wings began to move, beating the wind into submission, as they soared upward, bursting from the cavern's walls that had held them captive.

They flew over their land and they saw the great lands of Duradane, its beauty, its strife from war, its soldiers fighting to regain its peace and drive out those who had robbed them of their freedom. The dragon began to fly higher and higher. The air suddenly became cold with thick clouds swirling around them. It was as if the sky had opened up and swallowed them, sending them soaring into another dominion. The earth below was now unfamiliar. Jemma began to cry, but her brother pulled her closer to comfort her. As they continued to fly higher and higher, the land was no longer visible.

There came to them, a sweet, alluring and comforting smell...intoxicating. The clouds continued to swirl around their heads and their minds became calm, quiet, seemingly being invited into a pleasant

slumber. They listened to nothing but the *flap....*
flap...flap of the creature's wings beating the air to stay
in flight, both children being lulled into an inviting,
bewitching sleep.

When the children awoke in the land of
Swindalia, they found themselves resting in a field of
flowers, the sweet aroma of Sweet Anne's Lace, Baby's
Breath, Lilac and other species of flowers unfamiliar to
the children.

"This must have been what we smelled when we
were riding on Jade's back. Oh, aren't they beautiful?"
exclaimed Jemma.

With a new burst of energy, she jumped up and
began to run around feeling free and alive, stopping
only to pick the beautiful flowers, one by one
examining and smelling their sweet, innocent scent.

The trees and forest surrounding this beautiful
meadow had the look and feel of a changing season.
The leaves held sadness, as if to convey a last dying
attempt to pronounce their beauty. While the leaves
were turning to brilliant splashes of color, one could
also see the rugged hues of browns, a sign of a dying
season. The land's vegetation was like spring, summer
and fall, all expressed at once.

"Jemma, come on. We have to find Jade."

Jemma dropped her flowers and ran to catch up

with her brother. Standing just a few feet away, was Jade, waiting for the children to awaken. Jade was easily seen, standing at the forest's edge guarding the two small humans while they slept. As Jemma and Frederick came to Jade, Frederick noticed that Jade was looking up. There upon a large tree was a carving on its trunk.

"I believe that this is our first clue to lead us to the locket and the key," Jade said, as he studied the strange carving on the trunk of the tree.

"You mean you don't already know where these things are?" Frederick asked, surprised by this obvious revelation.

"There are many things about this land that neither you nor I know. Why do I know of some things and not others? Perhaps this may have been part of the curse on me? I do not know. There are creatures of many kinds here and we will have to seek out and solve many riddles to find our treasure. This will not be an easy task, but it is the task that has been laid before you. You must choose how you will face this challenge. You must be brave. I am your friend and I will help you in every way that I can," encouraged Jade.

"Wait a minute...did you say challenge before 'you'? We can't do this; we're here to help you! We have no idea what we are doing!" said Jemma in a panic.

"What does the clue say, Jade? It appears to be in an unfamiliar script," asked Frederick.

"Know where to go; this is no place to be slow,
Your mission is simple, but beware of the ripple
Of time and space and all who are in this place.
To find the key and the locket,
look in your pocket.
Your journey is long, but beware;
There may be a song or a phrase that will lead you
astray and allow dismay.
Next, see the map buried within the sap."

Frederick quickly slipped his hand into his four inch deep pocket and pulled out what looked to be a picture of a river with a paddle boat beside it. The river was illustrated to look very wide.

"Okay, this is weird! How did this get into my pocket? Jade please answer me. What do you expect us to do?" Frederick asked, more than a little perplexed.

"This would appear to be the first task. I doubt seriously that this clue will take us to our final destination. It would appear that you must cross the river to get a little further toward the key and the locket. It says there is a map buried in the sap. Do you suppose that is meant literally?" asked Jade.

"There's a lot of that sticky stuff on the other side of the tree," said Jemma.

She swerved around the tree and sunk her hand into a sticky, wet glob of resin on the trunk of this magnificent tree. As she started to scrape the sap away, a small map of Swindalia was being revealed. She pulled the piece of linen containing the map from the sticky goop and   looked at it with a bit of curiosity. There was a palace right in the middle of the map.

"Jade, what is that?" inquired Jemma.

"Ah, yes, the Court Jester's Palace. This is where we must go to face Banion," answered Jade.

"I thought you didn't know anything," said Frederick.

"I don't! It says 'Court Jester Banion's Palace right here! See?" Jade responded.

"Oh! There's the river right there. See on the map? It looks like we are really close. I think we can walk from here," said Frederick.

"And just how else did you plan to get there?" asked Jade.

"Fly, of course!" said Frederick and Jemma simultaneously.

"You are a dragon. You flew us here. Why can't you fly there?" asked Jemma.

"I could fly, but we have to be careful, as there are those who would attempt to stop us from completing our journey. If we walk, we are better able to hide. We must stay off of the main roads and paths. Travel only during the day. From the map it would appear that it will take us two or three days. While safety is important, time is also critical. We must not tarry," pushed Jade.

Soon the three of them were on their way. They

had a destination, but how they would get there was unclear; a path, a road? And all of them were thinking about this 'map'. *Was it trustworthy? Who would have put it there? Were they expected? If so, how?* But they knew that they had to find the locket and the key. There was no turning back now if the White Wizard was correct. There was no going back at all without their prize.

It was a cool day, much like fall in Duradane. The leaves on the trees were adorned with colors as though the tops of these lovely giants were the tips of paint brushes; red, yellow, gold and so many colors in between. The colors were vibrant and vivid, displaying every imaginable hue of the rainbow. The smell of the forest held the aromas and sounds of autumn.

As they walked upon the decaying carpeted foliage, the loud crunching under foot reminded the children of the games they played back home with the fall leaves. They used to pile them all up and then take turns jumping into the pile. It was amazingly funny to watch each other, as he or she would emerge with leaves sticking out from all over....their hair, their clothes, in between their fingers. They remembered using the colorful leaves to decorate for the coming festival they had every year.

From the open field, they began to walk into this strange land. There was a hush that made them feel uneasy, yet they knew that they had to continue. Jade stopped abruptly.

"Wait. Listen!" Jade whispered. "Do you hear something? I think we are being followed...watched. Once we get deeper into the forest, we need to establish some landmarks. Don't forget that we may have to come back the same way."

"How do we do that...leave marks for us to get back? Won't others see them?" asked Frederick.

"I guess the best thing would be to make our own carvings in the trees or find a guide...someone we can trust," answered Jade.

"I'm not thinking that your last option is going to happen right away, Jade," said Jemma.

"Wait...," Frederick piped up. "I have my pocket knife. Luckily it was in my pocket when I grabbed my pants before leaving home."

So, they agreed to make small, indiscreet markings, just big enough to allow them to find their way out. They traveled on, following the map directions and only stopping for short rests along the way. Each of them was dealing in silence with their own fear and trepidation, as they walked onward. The children were feeling the effects of having not had any food for many hours and they were beginning to weaken. Hours continued to pass, as did the daylight itself.

As they came to a small clearing in the woods Jade said, "I hear water." The other two smiled.

"That's good, right?" asked Frederick.

"I don't know," answered Jade. "I think that it might be a stream cut between some rocks and trees, possibly leading to a river...that would be my guess. Do you think you two can go just a little be farther? Let's try to find the source of the stream and then we can rest for the night."

The children agreed to go on, trying hard to find the energy to go just another step, then another, and another. They had put their complete trust in this creature who had taken them away from their homeland and all that was familiar.

The terrain was beginning to change and within the hour Jade saw signs of water, rocks, muddy ground, and more rocks that seemed to lead them into the area of a creek bed. Throughout the journey, the children shared with Jade the happenings in the cave and what the White Wizard had told them.

"Here, children, let's rest here. We are close enough to some water and I will go get some food. Stay out of site...keep yourselves safe. I will return shortly," declared Jade.

"Jade, what if something happens to you?" asked Jemma, fearing being left alone.

"My dear child, you must have faith. Be brave. I will not desert you. Now rest while you can and I will bring nourishment for you."

Jemma and Frederick looked around and found a clump of bushes. They snuggled in amongst the brush to hide themselves and rest. Jade began to walk away, but took one last look at the two small people that he had grown to care so much about, knowing that the true hope for success on this mission lay on their shoulders. As he left their sight, he took to the sky flying only high enough to cover the area more quickly, but low enough to stay hidden.

This scouting trip would help Jade get a little better idea of the landscape and find food to gather. This land was plentiful and there seemed to be an abundance of berries, mushrooms, and herbs. The herbs would help to satisfy hunger and give energy to their consumers.

Dawn was coming fast. Jemma and Frederick were squirming, waking up from having slept soundly the entire night. Jade had returned with a wide assortment of foods. They wasted no time devouring it and filling themselves to satisfaction.

"Are you ready to continue?" asked Jade.

Both nodded their heads and made the mark on a nearby tree, their map for the way home.

As the days and nights passed, the terrain continued to became wet, soggy and rocky, with less concentrated forest; meaning fewer areas in which to hide. They had found their way to a creek. Water was flowing more freely assuring them that they were on the right track to the river.

Every now and then, Jade would stop and look around side, to side, front to back, feeling the presence of another nearby.

Riddles for the Kingdom

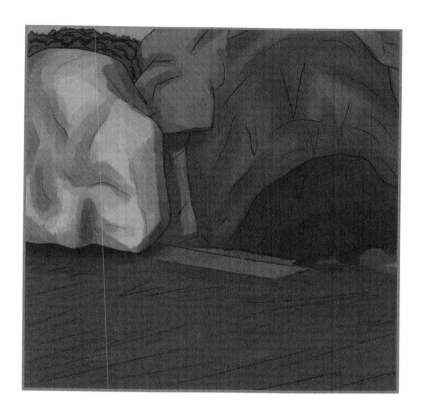

Pen It! Publications, LLC

Chapter 7

*J*ade did not want to frighten the children, but the ever present feeling of someone or something following them drove him to take as many precautions as possible. It was imperative that they continue moving at a fast pace. It was vital that if they were attacked that they be able to protect themselves. While there had been no living being in sight except the three of them, Jade was keenly aware of another's presence.

Suddenly, racing in front of them, was a large hawk-like creature with a loud piercing cry! He flashed across their paths nearly knocking Frederick down. Jade spread his wide wings in front of the two innocent children to protect them, while letting out his own piercing cry, along with a streak of fire in the direction of the attacking creature. Again, the predator charged the invaders, protecting the boundaries of its territory. More 'hawks' began to accompany this single attacker. The sky became black with the bird-like beings, threatening even the fire breathing Jade.

Just when they thought there was no hope to escape, arrows began to splinter through the sky and into the invading birds. As the flying creatures fell to the ground dead, they appeared to transform. They bore the tattooed mark upon their arm of the Seltons. These creatures were goblin-like with the objective to kill.

There was no sigh of relief from the three outsiders. Even though they had been saved, the questioned remained: *How did they all know that the three of them were coming?* It was almost as though the two forces, the birds and the ones responsible for the arrows, were fighting each other for the children and Jade.

Who were these creatures whose arrows saved them from a certain ill fate? As quickly as the arrows appeared, stillness and perplexity abandoned Jade and the children. No one was there; no one came to talk with them. It was as if the trees themselves had shot those arrows.

Jade and the children stood speechless for what seemed to be a long time. Jade kept thinking that the owners of the arrows would come to them and talk, or maybe capture them. Nothing happened.

Jade finally spoke, "Are you both alright?"

Both nodded, still too shocked to speak.

The sudden realization that Jade's suspicions were confirmed and that they were not alone motivated him to push the children onward. However, Jade was keenly aware of eyes watching... watching...watching...

"Let's keep moving. Can you do it?" asked the dragon.

"Lead the way," said Jemma.

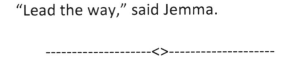

Day after day, they dragged along the rocky, muddy and uneven path. After a while, even the beautiful vibrant leaves and flowers began to dull. The map had already been misleading. This journey was taking more than a couple of days. Jade kept hearing a ticking noise in his head, a constant reminder that time would eventually run out and he didn't know if they were getting close or not. As they pushed forward, they began to notice a thunderous rushing sound added to their surroundings. Yet, everyone ignored it, as it grew ever so gradually.

Frederick looked up from staring at his torn, wet boots, finally aware of his soaked and bone-chilling clothes. There was a patch of blue and white in the distance. With his concentration on the mysterious object, he didn't see where he was going. It was then that he tripped over a tree root, slipped on the rock and fell to the ground.

"Frederick! Are you alright?" exclaimed Jemma in a worried, shaky voice. She too was getting tired and dropped to the ground next to her brother. Jade even seemed to have an exhausted look on his face.

"How can we go on? I just can't, Frederick...I just can't," Jemma cried sounding defeated, going into a panic that she had not experienced since the very first night.

"Come on, little ones. We must not stop," Jade encouraged gently, but in a husky whisper. He knew he had pushed them. These brave children had grown to trust him and depend on him, in spite of all uncertainty.

Then Jade notice that Frederick was indeed looking at something; something he thought he might never see.

"The RIVER!!!" Jade cried out.

Jemma pulled her head up and began to run towards the blue and white blur. Jade and Frederick followed. As the sound of the rushing water became louder and almost deafening, they arrived at the edge that would prove to be a turning point in their journey. The great rushing water was a rapid of power, engulfing anything in its path. The river was a mighty giant, daring them, laughing at them to intrude its boundaries.

"How will we get to the other side?" yelled Frederick, trying to speak above the noise of the water.

"Look! There is a boat, the one from the riddle...it has to be!" exclaimed Jemma.

"NO! It's a trick; Wait!" Jade rebuked as he swung his large dragon's tail around pushing the boat from the ledge into the river. The three stood there watching as the only obvious way to get across the river was being thrown away. As the boat began to slide into the angry jaws of the river, the river began to transform into an angry monster.

Pen It! Publications, LLC

The water changed from small rapids tripping over the rocks to large waves of white walls fighting and crashing into each other and trampling anything in its path....including breaking the boat into millions of little pieces like matchsticks. They all stood astonished. As the boat was finally digested by the monster before their eyes, the river calmed to the rushing pace it had been when they had first approached it. Jade had indeed saved them from an undesirable fate. They all had the same thought; was there a curse on this place?

"How did you know?" asked Frederick, barely audible and still staring as though mesmerized by the river's power.

"I didn't know for sure, but there is an evil feeling around this place; do you feel it? The boat was too easy, too unsafe in the monstrous rushing water ahead of us. There has to be another clue to help us find another way across."

The trio began to look around for clues, another riddle or something that would help them. The water had calmed, but still was roaring and loud as it raced to its destination.

The hope that had sparked so much joy had been snatched away as quickly as it had come. Jemma and Frederick's spirits were suddenly and most visibly fading. Thoughts of defeat were again running back into their thoughts like an old adversary crowding out any desire to keep going.

"I don't see anything," complained Jemma. She felt hopelessness that possessed her like a spell.

Helpless, she sat down against a rock and just waited, staring into oblivion. The sound of the rushing water, the smell of the muddy ground, moldy and lifeless, the cold rock she now sat upon seemed to make her part of the scenery, not a hero. There was no hope and no place to go. She was resigning herself to their defeat.

The other two worked diligently to find an answer, but to no avail. They too were exhausted and sat down.

Jade tried to think...*Should I fly across the river? Dare I chance it?*

All at once Jemma spied something. Pointing her finger to an unclear place in the rocky side of the hill, she said, "What is that, Jade?" She got up and walked toward a rock continuing to point at what looked to be an inscription. "Look, it is the language that was on the first clue. What does it say, Jade?"

"Read it!" exclaimed Frederick.

Jemma wiped off the dirt that shielded some of the letters and watched intently as Jade began to read:

Dark is the path you must go through.
When once you unlock the secret to my tomb,
Down, down, down you must go.
The path leads under and not over.
That which you seek is on the other side.
Say the words, 'We come in Peace,'
And my secret will be revealed unto you.
Beware if you are not a friend, for the path

Will lead you to your end.

"What does this mean?" asked Jemma, her brother nodding his head as though he were asking the same question.

"Somehow we have to communicate that we mean no harm and I don't know if the ground will open up or if the rocks will fall or the river will part but we must try or we will never know," Jade answered contemplating what to do.

"We Come in Peace!" commanded Jade.

With these words, the large stone with the inscription on it began to move away, opening its large barrier into a dark hidden cavern, stairs leading to who knows where, but down...down...down."

Chapter 8

As the three companions looked with amazement into the dark, scary place, they held their breath, not knowing what might happen next...who or what might be lurking in the cave; who or what might come jumping out at them?

Jemma and Frederick looked at each other as if to say, 'We don't really have to go into another cave, do we?'

They knew, of course, that this was exactly where they had to go. The stone's movement stopped, allowing a silent invitation into its opening. Without further thought, Jade began to approach the entrance. With one last glance at each other, the trio entered. It was rather narrow and not very high. Jade found himself slouching and turning sideways in order to get through. There was a musty smell within this place and the evidence of water was present, the sound of drip, drip, dripping was echoing in the hollow chamber.

As they began to walk further down the dark steps, the entrance behind them slammed shut. Blackness was all around them and the two children clung to their monstrous companion for safety. Once again, they found themselves with no other choice than to go forward. Jade noticed that along the wall was a lantern that simply needed to be lit.

With a gentle puff from his fiery nostrils, the torch was lit, providing light to guide their way. Down, down, down they walked, hearing only the tapping of their steps on the stone stairs. The dripping water and their hearts that were beating rapidly. The noises inside the heads of the children were deafening. Fear of the unknown swelled within them with each step they took. Jade did not pay attention to the distractions but continued to move downward through the shadows that accompanied them by the single light he held.

As the trio continued their journey, the stairs became even more steep, winding around and around into a downward spiral. The three intruders glued their backs to the wall sliding one foot over, one step to another. The wall was cold, hard, and wet. It took seemingly forever to reach what appeared to be the bottom of the stairs, where the cave opened into a large room. The air was close, humid and still. The oxygen was thin, making it difficult to breath anything but short rapid breaths. The children became light headed and faint. They could now hear the river rushing above them and realized that they were standing directly under the river.

Along the perimeter of the room were long troughs that reached from their side of the room to the other side. The troughs were filled with a liquid. The light from the lantern that Jade held, shimmered upon the trough's contents. Their guess was that the liquid was oil. Jade breathed his fire upon it and they all watched the oil ignite, its light running to get to the other side of the room. They could now see what was before them. As the light poured over the room, it created a trigger that started a motorized-like movement of the objects in the room.

In front of them were several large round ball-like obstacles with spikes protruding from them. Each of these round obstacles were suspended from the ceiling by large chains. As the light now surrounded them, these chains began to swing back and forth, one going one direction and the other going the opposite direction. As they swung together, they would nearly touch. This action continued to increase in speed and intensity. They noticed in silence that there was not just one row of these obstacles to pass but six rows between them and the other side of the room. All were working in opposition to each other. To get through these would require agility and timing, not to mention luck. Since the chains were attached to the ceiling, it was not possible for even Jade to fly up and over it and because of his size, there would be no getting through it or under it.

"Oh, my!" muttered Frederick under his breath. "What next?"

"Let's consider this for a moment, my friends," said Jade "We can either try to go through this or figure out a way to stop the movement."

Jade continued to think, studying the movement

of the chains and the balls that were attached. "Okay, children, this is what we are going to do. Get on my back."

"What are we going to do, Jade? This can't be good," said Frederick, trying so very hard to be brave...to be a *man*. Jemma just looked too frightened to speak.

Without any further discussion, Jade heaved the children onto his back and leaped to the first chain as far up as he could and began to move from chain to chain in well-orchestrated movements. As the balls approached below him he would leap to the next chain.

Jemma was screaming, Frederick was yelling, "AAAAAAAAAHHHHHHHH! WAIT! STOP! OH, NO! JAAAAAADE! WATCH OUT!" But, Jade continued winding through the puzzle, concentrating on only the movements of the chains before him until at last they reached the other side. They dropped to the ground, falling, relieved and ALIVE.

"Can this get any worse?" asked Frederick.

"It just did," answered Jemma, pointing her finger at what appeared to be another puzzle that they would have to work through.

"Don't move children," warned Jade.

On the floor in front of them was what looked to be a large checkerboard. It looked like tiles that you could just walk across, but for the warning that Jade had given.

Jade found a small stone on the floor and picked

it up. "Watch."

And he tossed it onto the tiled floor. When it hit the first tile, skipping across, a spear plunged upward ready to pierce anything that might have been standing there. The spear pushed itself up until it met its twin protruding from the ceiling. As Jade and the two children stood there in awe, they could only hear the clanking of the two pieces of metal hitting each other, the sound echoing in the dungeon over and over as if to continue to give a reminder of its warning.

"Now what, Jade, how can we pass over this?" inquired Jemma. "Someone really doesn't want us to get through here."

"There has to be a way. Let me think on this a moment. The riddle above said to enter only if you are a friend...say the words." And with this thought, Jade deepened his voice, and uttered a loud and commanding again, "WE COME IN PEACE!"

At once, the spikes retracted, the checkerboard floor began to sink while another floor from the side walls pushed together offering a new and safe floor on which to walk.

"You did it, Jade! You did it!" the children exclaimed with excitement.

"Wait..." Jade picked up another stone and skipped it across the newly presented floor. Too their relief, the stone made tapping noises across the floor and landed in silence.

"I guess there is some good still here in this place. Someone is determined to protect something.

So I would say that we have allies here somewhere...we just have to find them and figure out how to trust each other.   Until then, we need to keep moving, ok, Jemma? Ok Frederick? Time is passing and if we tarry too long, we will not be able to find the way out."

Jade, Jemma and Frederick continued to walk on, crossing the newly laid floor and forward into the only opening ...a tunnel. Water was over their feet and the dripping was more like raining. The tunnel wound around a curve coming to a dead end except for another set of stairs.   There was no stopping or standing around for discussion.

This was their only way out. Hopefully it would lead them out on the other side of the river. Jade took the lead, then Frederick, followed up by Jemma. As Jemma neared the first of many steps she looked down and notice something shiny coming from under the step. She reached down and picked up the object.

"Look. Is this something we need?" She pulled out a long interwoven chain, which held a locket. "Look how beautiful!"

Both of her companions turned to look at what she had found. "Oh, dear child," whispered the dragon. "You have found part of what we need! And we almost walked right by it! Ha ha!" They all started to laugh, not because it was funny, but at their relief.

As the dragon looked upon the intricate shiny locket he said, "Place it around my neck, Jemma. It will be safe there. For us to have found it would suggest that it wanted to be found." As he touched it, he could feel the goodness from whose hands had welded this precious treasure.

"There is magic that surrounds this locket," Jade said. "Now we need only to find the key to unlock it and set me free."

He looked up at the dark steps and another torch that had been placed in a bracket on the wall. Again with a puff from his nostrils, the torch was ignited, giving them a light to their path and shadowy companions on the wall. Jade nodded his head toward the steps and they began their tedious climb, hearing the now familiar dripping of the water and the tapping of their feet as they walked up the cold hard steps. The stairs were uneven making it difficult to keep their footing. Jade again was forced to crouch down to fit through the narrow passage.

"Frederick, can you hold the torch? I am afraid that trying to get this big body of mine through this place I will lose my footing and fall and lose the torch."

"Sure!" Frederick liked it when he was being asked to help.

As the large crouching dragon turned to hand the torch to Frederick, his foot slipped, missing Frederick's hands, dropping the torch to the floor. It tumbled top to bottom snuffing out the only light they had.

Blackness consumed them. There was no torch to help light their way out of this chasm.

"I'm sorry!" exclaimed Frederick sounding

ashamed for not catching the light.

"No, I'm sorry, Frederick! It was my fault," said Jade remorsefully.

"Is everyone okay?" asked Jemma. "Let's keep moving. The sooner we get to the top, the sooner we will not have to worry about the torch."

The stairway was steep, uneven and difficult to maneuver. The children's only guide was to keep stepping up…up…up…guiding themselves by dragging their hands along the cold, damp wall….turning, turning, turning through the spiral staircase that led them to freedom.

Jade felt the narrowness of the passage becoming more and more difficult to get through. Again it took what seemed like a long time to climb. The air was still stale and difficult to breath. But Jade continued to push them and to encourage them.

"Only a little bit farther. You can do this. You are strong and brave. Who would have guessed that a year ago that you would have such an adventure?"

In spite of Jade's prodding, the children didn't feel very brave. In fact, they were exhausted and wanted right now to just go home and get into their nice warm beds and lay their heads upon their wonderfully soft feather pillows. They found themselves thinking of their mother and father, where they might be and if they were even alive. *We must push on,* they both thought to themselves. *We can't go backwards.*

Pen It! Publications, LLC

Continuing to climb, they began to once again notice faint glimpses of light sneaking in from somewhere. These small bits of light drew them onward. The light was the hope and the motivation they needed.

The three companions reached the top of the stairs. The light rushed in through every crevice and pin hole, sneaking in from behind the closed door. As light broke through the darkness, hope empowered them. However, the closed door barred them from escape. Vines grew all over the door, suggesting this space had not been approached in a very long time.

Jade and Frederick reached up to grab the vines and free the door from its webbed fingers of entrapment. As Frederick took hold of a group of vines, they began to move, their strength pulling away from his grasp and turning upon him. The vines began to crawl off of the door and to reach for both of the children. The spindly fingers moved with amazing rapidity and engulfed Jade as well. The vines moved to wrap around arms, legs and whatever they could, encasing the children; there was nowhere to hide, nowhere to go.

Jemma and Frederick, becoming restricted by their movements began to panic. While Jade was pinned against the wall by vines around him, his head was still free. He took a deep breath and let go of a large fireball that exploded at the base of the vine forcing a retreat, and letting go of the captives. Again, Jade breathed his heat upon the door itself, charring right through its center.

"Quickly, children, let's move," said Jade.

They stepped through the opening and into the bright light, their vision diminished from having been in the dark for so long. But their hearing was still very much intact. There before them was an army of soldiers. As their eyes quickly adjusted they saw the soldiers, swords and arrows drawn.

Chapter 9

The light was blinding at first. But Frederick and Jemma could not mistake the feeling of the sharp point that pressed against them after stepping through the door. Their eyes adjusted to see an army of defenders waiting for them. These soldiers were short in stature, muscular, with peculiarly pointed ears and slanted eyebrows.

"Who dares to pass?" a voice erupted from the crowd of strangers.

"We come in peace, my friend," said Jade. "We seek no trouble, but only to find the key to this locket," Jade said lifting the locket up to be seen. "We seek to rid an evil spell that has been put upon me and has allowed evil to come to our homeland."

"Where do you come from?" asked one from the crowd.

"Duradane," answered Jade. "We need to complete our mission and return there, as soon as possible. As I said, we mean you no trouble. May we pass?"

A ranking officer spoke up, "We will need to consult our Council first. Until then you must come with us. We are known as the Tree Elves from the house of Ananon. Our land has become corrupted as well. It started when a human...a Court Jester, it is said, came to our land. We were forced to build our homes in the trees and let the forest grow up around us for protection. Our community is trying to preserve some goodness in our part of this land. We saw you when the goblins attacked you, before you got to the river. Our people were the ones that saved you. We have been watching you throughout your journey."

"Why didn't you reveal yourselves before now? And why do you feel that you have to hold us up from our journey with swords and arrows?" asked Jade.

Another Elf spoke up. "The only way that we could know for sure that you had come in peace was to see if you were able to solve the riddles. The riddles are enchanted. The spell prevents them from revealing themselves to those with evil in their hearts. My name is Ananon. I am the King of the Tree Elves. Come, return with us to our homes where we can eat and drink. We can discuss how best to proceed," said the Elf leader.

Jade knew there was no need to argue but remained skeptical at the thought of sharing a plan to 'proceed.' The Elves lowered their weapons but did not remove their pressing eyes from them. It was a human that brought ill upon their people and now there were two more humans....and a dragon!

There hadn't been a dragon in this land for many years. Some of the soldiers were young enough that they had never seen a real dragon before. Neither the

Elves nor the trio were comfortable trusting the other. But Jade and the children followed the leader in silence, as the tribe led them back to their homes. Jade and the children looked up into the trees, unable to see anything but vegetation.

As they continued to walk, they began to see some movement from above, revealing beautifully constructed homes built in the high branches of the trees. Rope bridges swung from place to place allowing inhabitants to maneuver and survive without coming to the ground.

Walking closer to the tree city's entrance, Ananon began to speak, telling about their people, how they had once lived in peace in fair lands and pastures. Ananon told them how the Jester came and how his people had been forced up into the trees. They had been in hiding for quite some time. But he, as King, held hope of the resolution of evil and restoration of his people. He had continued to wait for a sign, something that would tell him when to rebel and take back their lands.

Much of the King's story mirrored Jemma and Frederick's, a peaceful land taken over by an evil lord. Jade and the children found themselves listening intently for hours about the history of these magnificent people. Even after they had arrived at Ananon's home where food and water were served, they continued to talk, comparing stories and experiences.

The hour became late and the children, trying very hard not to go to sleep, were overcome and lost the battle. Both Jemma and Frederick, sitting on either side of Jade, had fallen against him succumbing to the power of sleep. Their bellies were full, they were warm, dry, and for the first time in a very long time, they felt safe.

"Master Jade, let us retire for the evening," said Ananon. "My keepers will show you to your rooms and help you with the children. We are all tired and will make our plans for proceeding with your journey tomorrow. We are your friends to aid you however we can." Ananon turned and left while the keepers assisted Jade in getting the children to bed.

Pen It! Publications, LLC

Chapter 10

*J*emma awoke early. The morning's peaceful beginning tempting her to roll over and go back to sleep. She lay in bed listening to the sounds of this new day. She loved to do that at home, hearing the Whip-poor-will's call in the mornings, feeling the coolness of the early spring morning breeze sneaking in the open window and brushing across her. Then the sparrows would wake up and join the songs of the other birds. She opened her eyes. Through the open window, which was shaded by sheer curtains, shone the sun. It was just beginning to reveal itself over the horizon, sharing its dim light within the room and with the new day.

This had been the first restful night's sleep since before their house had been burned and their parents taken. Her muscles ached from sleeping so hard and long. Jemma reached up to rub her eyes removing the 'matter' from them, blinking wildly to see more clearly the room in which she had slept.

Jade was nowhere in the room. In a bed beside her was her brother, still asleep, breathing heavily and deeply. How nice it was to feel safe, to see Frederick resting. He was such a wonderful brother. He did take good care of her even when he was scared himself.

For a brief moment it made Jemma feel a little guilty for fighting with him like she used to do at home. *It was all meant innocently and after all, isn't that what siblings did?*

This brief thought escaped her, as though it had been whisked away in the wind, replaced by her observation of the room. She noticed just how big this room was. It was all white: walls, floor and ceiling. Around the perimeter of it were large round pillars that stretched from floor to ceiling set out from the walls just enough to provide a walkway and spaced about 6 feet apart.

The room itself was rather sparse. There was only the beds in the room and a few pictures hanging on the walls between the pillars, displaying older elves that may or may not have occupied this dwelling. Jemma looked intently at the pictures, studying them. For a brief moment she thought that she heard them speak to her…soft, gentle, quiet voices discussing something about the enemy.

She blinked a couple of times and shook her head from side to side, trying to snap herself out of this illusion. Her eyes roamed to observe other parts of the room. To the left of her bed was the large open window, the sheers hung from ceiling to floor, still wistfully moving from the incoming breeze. Jemma stepped out of her bed onto the cold white marble floor and walked to the window.

The view was breathtaking. Below her were the

courtyards and bridges, different levels of them connecting and interwoven like the artistry of a spider's web. There was the brief whiff of bacon frying coming through the air. No one can disguise that smell! Her stomach began to growl.

Across the way, in another tree house, she spotted the Elf King speaking with Jade. She watched in silence, trying to savor this peaceful moment. She didn't know when another peaceful time would come or if they would survive the next part of their journey. The future was unknown.

Entranced in the confines of her own thoughts, she heard a knock on the door. Frederick sat up with a start. He was ready to jump on whatever it was that was coming at him. The knock came again.

"Yes, who's there?" Jemma answered in a shy barely audible voice.

Again, through the door came a knock, only this time with a voice.

"My name is Toron. I am a council member for King Alanon. He has requested your presence, along with your dragon friend. Be swift in your preparation. There is much to do. I will wait here and escort you to the King."

"We will be right with you," said Jemma, taking charge, allowing Frederick to wake up more fully.

"Jemm, what is going on?"

"I don't know Frederick. I have been awake for a while and have been watching out the window. Jade is already with King Ananon. I have no idea how long they have been there. I don't even remember going to bed!"

"Me either!" replied Frederick.

"Come look," Jemma said, waving Frederick out of bed to the window.

"Maybe they are discussing our next plan. We have help now. Hurry! Let's get dressed and go find out what they are going to do," said Jemma.

Toron waited impatiently, pacing first one direction then another, until the children would join him. Toron was a loyal Elf, but at times seemed short tempered and impatient with circumstances that he obviously could not change. The children finally came out of their room, dressed and ready to go. Toron eyed them, as though he just didn't quite trust them, after all, they were human. So was that awful beast that came and took over their land. He was old enough to remember. However, feelings aside, Toron led the way and they approached King Ananon, who was in deep conversation with Jade. They were sitting upon the steps that led into another house in the trees.

"Good morning, children," greeted the King.

The children gracefully bowed with a nod and reply, "Good morning, Sire." Having been raised in a kingdom themselves, they had been taught proper manners when going before a King.

"I have been discussing with Jade how we should proceed and what would be the best plan of attack."

Jemma and Frederick exchanged looks with Jade, the children accepting Jade's nod of approval. This King was now on a mission, no longer waiting for the 'sign'. The presence of Jade and his companions was that sign. The Elves had prepared for many years, strengthening their armies and strategies. They sought to overcome that which had been stolen from their lives, their homes, and their freedoms. These people were very resourceful as well. They had taken what seemed to be nothing and made a glorious dwelling. It had to be magic; so mysterious was this place.

Frederick wanted to ask them so many questions but chose to sit down in silence, hushed by the seriousness of the matter at hand. Also present were several other Elves. Many of them were wearing armor. These must have been the army leaders.

Frederick and Jemma went over to sit beside the King as others continued to gather. There must have been around 20 altogether. Each one, when approaching the King, bowed before him, and then quickly found a place to sit.

"We are gathered here on this morning of hope," began the King. "Yesterday we were bid the good fortune of being united with allies, friends who are seeking the trophy of peace. Allow me to make the introductions of our guests to you and of you to them. The man child beside me is Frederick of Duradane and his sister, Jemma sits beside him. These young children have been given the task to restore order to both our land and their own. This dragon, Jade, who has been cursed, was changed from his true nature. Jade's hope is to find, along with the locket that he wears around his neck, the key to unlock the spell. This spell has affected us all, leaving not only our lands in the hands of evil, but also their homeland of Duradane, in the same fate," explained the King.

The King turned to Jade, Jemma and Frederick. "This is my Council, my friends. We work together as a group to discuss and figure out how to fight our enemies; how to protect our people. The leader of my army is Lament. He has led our forces through many battles and continues to be my comrade and trusted friend. Beside him sits his senior officers, all of whom help us in our battle plans. They are excellent marksmen and train our defenders to be equally accurate. The remaining attendees are members of my Council. While I, as King have to make the final decisions and promote the strategies, I find that those who serve our people have important perspective and ideas to contribute. That is why I have gathered all of you together. Today is a new day! A day to conquer! A day to begin our lives as free People!"

The Council and guests enthusiastically applauded the King's words. This moment was one to remember and savor...a moment of history for all the people. As the cheering and yelling of their agreement began to die down, the King began to outline the strategies which he and Jade had proposed. They all knew that they would have to invade the castle and get past Banion.

King Ananon began by directing everyone's eyes to the large land map of Swindalia. The land was somewhat treacherous, in that it had hills and valleys which bordered the Elves' forest. The terrain looked beautiful. It reminded Jemma and Frederick of their homeland or at least the home that they once knew.

On the other side of the hills and valleys there appeared to be a desert area. This area was dangerous, as Banion had ordered a curse upon it. A curse was placed on the desert area by the Wizard Froc long ago. In this desert, an area wasteland, there were areas of quicksand, poisonous reptiles, and curses of evil hallucinations by whoever entered its borders. Jade knew that he would not be able to fly over this desert, as he would be too easily detected by the guards of Banion. In all of these years, Banion had taken time to make his plans and build his armies. Fear ran through this land, as the Seltons dominated all the territories from the desert's edge to the coastline.

Toron was first to speak after several moments of silence. Everyone looked up at the map and the seemingly impossible route to get to the castle where Banion lived.

"We have waited and trained for many years for this moment, but I see no possible way to reach it without all-out war in this God-forsaken land that lies between us and them. Look," Toron said, pointing to the map. "There is not only the desert to go through but alas, another river, one which we have not been to, one that doesn't recognize Elf magic. The river appears to be coming from the Martifita Mountains. These mountains are cold, treacherous, and snow is as deep as the trees are tall. We are so small in stature. How could we even walk on the snow or through it? And then, if we were to make it past that, we face the castle hidden somewhere around here," he pointed to the opening past the mountain range that appeared to open up to hills and valleys again, his face strained with concern. "The river appears to flow into the Sea of Goshen, where they say there are great whales and powerful sea animals. This is beyond my vision, beyond my knowledge and understanding," Toron said with dismay.

Upon hearing these words, the group was visibly discouraged. The map looked to be an impossible task, a death sentence. Toron, a respected veteran of the counsel, had given no hope or encouragement. Heads held low, the group felt visibly defeated.

Seeing this reaction, King Ananon spoke yet again, this time with a rather disapproving tone and disappointment, looking directly at Toron to address his comments.

"Oh, I see, Toron. So, you would be defeated before even trying? Before we even start? We finally have a chance to make a stand and take back our lands and you lose hope before we even start. You have given us good information about what we cannot do. And it is sure that Banion will not expect us to be successful this way. But, what if we are? It means the beginning of our beautiful world again, or it might mean even to die; but if we die, it will be with honor. We would die trying to destroy evil for good. Let us not think of what we cannot do, but work to create new solutions to encourage success. We are soldiers and defenders of Swindalia. We will do what we must. Our friends," Alanon looked up to address everyone, "have brought us what we need to succeed. And succeed we will! Now! Let's focus on what we CAN do! Who has some ideas...let's hear them."

Jade listened and contemplated what Toron said. There was much truth in what he said, but what if...just what if this map was inaccurate? Toron had said that much of this land beyond the borders of the Tree Elves was unfamiliar and "out of his sight". Maybe there was a hidden road around the desert. What if there was a boat at the river on the other side of the desert? Maybe this was the boat to which Frederick's map had been pointing. Maybe this was the river they must go through to find their way into the castle, not the other river leading to the Tree Elves.

"Where did this map come from? Are we sure that its land contour is true?" asked Jade.

"We have, for many years, sent out scouts to keep watch. The scouts returned this map a short time ago. They said that they found it. It was lying out on the desert floor, close to our borders like someone had dropped it," said the King.

"What if this map was intended to be found?

What if Banion's dragon dropped it on purpose? What if it is a ploy...what if...," Jade's words faded, as he realized his negative thoughts were unwelcome to the King.

"What if it's a trick?" Frederick spoke out to finish Jade's thought.

"Yes..." said King Ananon rubbing his chin between his fingers considering this thought.

"Let's assume that this was a trap and that Banion intended for us to come, hijacking us before we even get started. He knows that we are a proud people. I am sure that he has heard from his spies what we have been doing. Children, did anyone know that you had left your homeland when you came here? Did anyone see you?" asked the King. "His spies would have alerted him of this if so."

Jemma chimed in, with her faint but most assured voice, "NO...I don't think so. Before we found Jade in the cave, we had been running from the Seltons. But, that was after they had taken our parents away and burned our house. None of them saw us. We ran into the King's son and ..."

Jade jerked his head toward Jemma with a bewildering look upon his face. Why this alarmed him so, he did not know. He felt an odd connection with this man. "Why can't I remember?" Jade muttered to himself.

Jemma continued, "He was going to help us and take us to his encampment, when one of the trees that was cursed, I guess, picked him up and threw him. We thought him dead, but for the healing power of Jade."

"Where is this Prince now? Why did he not come with you?" asked Toron, still not convinced that they should trust these foreigners.

"After Jade healed him, he was put into a deep sleep. He is hidden in the cave from where we departed our land. He was not able to travel. Jade was driven here and...well...here we are," said Frederick.

"So, no one really saw you...no one knows that you exist?" asked another Elf.

"Well no...not the Seltons," said Fredrick. "None knew except our parents and they would have had no reason to have given us away, since we were not seen. For all our parents know, we are dead from the house fire. And for all we know of our parents, they are..." Frederick couldn't bring himself to verbalize the potential fate of his parents.

"Maybe we need to send some more scouts out and press onward and farther, in order to get better information," one of the generals suggested.

"Time is of the essence for us," Jade added. "If we fail to return to our world in a certain time frame, we will never be able to go back. I would not vote for this solution."

"How long do you have?" asked the General.

"I do not have an answer for that. Your time is a different continuum than our own. It is a gamble for us to even be here. Much of this information I was told when I first met the children. They had received this from a White Wizard who had come to watch over me while I was 'confined'...waiting for Jemma and Frederick to come to me," said Jade.

King Ananon listened intently and then said, "The strategies of war are like playing chess. Sometimes there are calculated risks and sometimes there are sure moves. I believe that in this case, we must take some calculated risks. Time is not on our side, but it is not something we have control of and not something we can determine. Therefore, we need to be diligent about our plans. We must strike with surprise, not be caught up in Banion's scheme. We will break up into three regiments. We will send one regiment up the middle," the King said as he pointed to the map, drawing an imaginary line from their own land through the desert and over the mountains.

"The second regiment will travel to the west," again drawing an imaginary line with his finger, "where they will scout as they go. If by chance they find a hidden road or byway, they will proceed toward the castle. The third regiment will go to the east," once again using his finger to draw the imaginary line around the eastern edge of the map, "to check for a way through to the other side. We must somehow get close enough to fight on Banion's turf and create enough diversion for the children to get into the castle. They will need time to look for and obtain the key. Their fate is our fate."

"Why must it be us to get the key? I know that

you are people of small stature. You said that yourself, but you are adults, experienced, brave and trained in battle. How can we, my sister and I, possibly accomplish such a task?" protested Frederick.

"Surely you can't be serious to expect us to face this horrible person, Banion," Jemma chimed in. "We have no knowledge of trickery or deceit. We are just children!"

Frederick paced back and forth in front of the sitting Council, his head down completely, resistant to any of this plan. He had always enjoyed pretending to be on adventures and Papa used to read him stories that he would act out. But, this was not just a story and certainly not a time for pretending. How could these people want to put him and Jemma in this kind of danger?

"How do you even get us there ...no way is clearly the sure way?"

The King walked over to Frederick, turned him to face him with both his hands resting upon the young boy's shoulders. There was an obvious grimace on Frederick's face as he looked to the ground in dismay.

The King was only about eight inches taller than the boy, but he was wise in his eyes and sure of what he needed to tell the boy and his sister. The King cupped Frederick's chin and pulled it up to look him in the eyes.

"Dear boy," the King began. "Do you remember yesterday when you arrived I spoke of a sign that we have been waiting for? Do you know why I trusted you so quickly? There are many spies in these lands, but it is only our people that know the legend to our past and to our future. Jade mentioned that we are in a different time continuum. In our land, our oppression has been upon us for 100 years. For you in your land it has been only months, correct?"

Frederick shook his head slightly to nod, yes!

The King continued, "In those 100 years, my people have prepared for this time when, after receiving the sign that was identified in our legend, we would be prepared militarily to fight. You are the answer to this legend. Listen to it!"

Ananon turned from the boy looking upward and began to recite the prophecy from his memory.

The lands of our fathers will be wrought with pain and dismay.
Your people will cry out for peace
but no one will hear.
The evil will progress and lives will be lost.

But upon this rock I will build a solid foundation, a hope,
a plan for justice and dominion over evil.

Two will come, though innocent and meek
They will be the key
as they face the evil in its dwelling place retrieving the truth for freedom.

Pen It! Publications, LLC

Their strength will come from their friend,
A third to come,
One who will be powerful,
One who would not be tamed,
One with a driving force to be in this land.

You will know this sign by the locket they possess.
Your mighty armies will again be strong
And the lands and its peoples will come together
as a mighty force.
Confidence will be restored and will belong to its true
inhabitants.

You are our hope, and our success. I know that this is much to place on a child's shoulders; a daunting task, but I believe that you truly are the coming of this prophecy," the King said.

"Forgive me, dear Lord, for stating the obvious, but you still haven't made it clear how we are going to get into the castle. With which regiment do we travel?" asked Frederick.

"Jade, do you have some insight? Toron, can you foresee this?" asked the King.

Toron concentrated, closed his eyes and wrinkled up his face, as if to try to see a blurred vision, more clearly. Then all at once, his face became relaxed, with eyes still shut, and a smile began to creep from the corners of his mouth.

Ahhhhh, yes Sire," announced Toron. "I believe

I see a glimpse of what will be. But, there are people who are unfamiliar with us. They look like us, but are tall and thin."

"Toron, those are the Grass Elves to the southeast of us," said the General. "They were once our allies, but have for many years moved into seclusion, in fear of Banion and his reign. Sire, we must call upon them for help," said the General. "With their help, we would have a mighty army."

"Okay, Toron," replied the King. "So, in your gift of foresight, you see us moving to the eastern border of the desert to find the way through with the help of the Grass Elves?"

"That would appear to be correct," encouraged Toron.

"General! Send out part of your scouting team to the east to alert our neighbors, the Grass Elves. Major Sorious, send out your scouts to the west for help. In that area there once was a company of Centaurs that were also allies with us. Perhaps they will help as well. Gentlemen, you have two days to return. Our mission begins then with or without the help of our friends. So do not tarry," warned the King.

"Gather your things and be on your way, scouts. The rest of us will do likewise. Gather food, weapons, and traveling necessities. Prepare our people for battle. With the prophecy coming to pass, a mighty effort to defeat our enemy begins," shouted King Ananon. "We will restore this land and its people."

A monstrous roar erupted from the crowd. As cheers and shouts continued, Jade remained quiet, standing by the Council. He was contemplating the plan and what he must ultimately do. The excitement of the crowd began to quiet to a few, who were talking amongst themselves. There was a new surge of hope, a belief that indeed they would be victorious in their quest.

Pen It! Publications, LLC

Chapter 11

The night before their journey brought with it a clear sky, with stars as plentiful as droplets of water in the ocean. It was beautiful, peaceful and hypnotic. Every little while, a star would ignite across the vast sky; a meteor burning bright, as it sketched its existence in the dark background.

While Jemma and Frederick had been there, they had become relaxed in their new environment. They had tried their best to help prepare for the journey, helping to gather and put together supplies with their new friends. The work was tiring and by evening, they were both exhausted. Having turned in for the night, Jade was left to ponder the coming events. He took this opportunity to stretch his wings and fly above the trees, to go out and feed before the next day.

While he flew through the quiet night, he could see beyond the trees. There was the edge of the desert. In the distance he saw the outline of another creature flying...another dragon, magnificent in color and size. For the first time he felt fear, fear for what he knew he must do. This dragon had to be Banion's dragon, Patarian. If Banion did not know the prophecy, he would not know of the children.

'If the children are to be successful, I must try to distract Banion. If I can engage Paterian, eyes will be on me, not them. Perhaps it will allow them to get through. I must go forth on my own,' Jade thought convinced of his fate.

Deep in thought, Jade found himself flying back to the shelter of the trees and to the room where the children slept. As he approached their room, he met Toron doing his nightly guard check.

"Good evening, Toron," Jade spoke first.

Toron nodded, a skeptical look on his face. "I was expecting you, Jade. Are you well?"

"I am fine, Toron. But, I have come to say goodbye to the children. My part of the quest takes me in a different direction."

"But, that is not part of the plan, Jade. The King is expecting you to travel with the children," Toron insisted.

"Yes, I know. But, it has occurred to me that by being a distraction to Banion and Patarian, the children's chances of passing undetected would be greater. I have just returned from my own scouting trip. Patarian waits for us. Banion's spies have succeeded in being alerted to our preparations. My plan is to engage Patarian. If I can draw him out and disable him, or better yet, kill him, Banion can't escape from his tower except to go through our forces that will be awaiting him."

Toron considered what Jade was saying. "I

should not tell you this, but because of your plan, I feel it is important to share some recent information from our scouts. Early this evening, our scouting party returned from the edge of our bordered forest. They reported seeing Banion riding Patarian. He was heading east, toward what we think is his castle. Banion is a Mad Man! But, he has no powers except from the Black Wizard, Froc, who is reportedly not here. Some talk about a Warlock King that drives him and is able to see beyond. If this Warlock King exists, it would be wise for you to block your thoughts so they cannot be seen. People in this world are deep in hiding, fearful of the Warlock and Banion's torment. What you plan is not going to be easy. But, I have to agree, that staging a distraction for the children to pass would make it more likely to be successful."

"I will look in on the children, but not wake them. Will you tell them, Toron, that I will see them again? I will meet them at the castle. Tell them to be brave, to persevere," encouraged Jade. "Peace be with you, Sir Toron. Watch after these younglings...trust them...they are strong, loving and wise beyond their years. They are the innocent in these times. I will leave shortly. Dawn is nearly here and I want to be gone before the others wake and light erupts."

"I wish you success, Master Jade. May the wind be always at your back and the sun bright to light your way before you." Toron gave his blessing not lightly but with thoughtful consideration. Jade bowed and turned to the open doors to take flight.

Pen It! Publications, LLC

Chapter 12

*T*he screeching of Patarian's arrival could be heard throughout the castle. As he entered the window of his master's chambers, Banion sat alone waiting for news that would impress upon him his next move.

"Patarian, what news have you brought me? Is it time to play? Oh, how I love the game of chess...he moves...then I move...Who is the wiser?" Banion laughed using his hands to gesture as though he were really playing chess.

Banion got up laughing and singing and skipping about, giddy as a school boy, excited about the war to come. This was nothing but a game to him. He was quite confident of his victory to come.

"What news do you bring me, my good dragon?"

"Scouts have been coming in and out of the forest for a long time. There is stirring about but none have yet crossed into the desert lands. I dropped the map, as you instructed and it has been taken," said Patarian.

"OH, MARVELOUS!" exclaimed Banion. "Our plan is under way. Once they come into the desert, we can make our stand and defeat them! Call out the Militia to be ready to march. We may need to call upon

Froc...although trying to get him back here would be a challenge. Call the Warlock King. I need his advice and consultation.

"Guard!" yelled Banion. "Summon Morpheus, the Warlock King! Now!"

Suddenly Banion's disposition changed from one of child's play to anger and torment. Even his servants feared his unpredictability. No one trusted him...not even his own dragon, Patarian.

The castle in which Banion dwelt was thousands of years old. There were three towers reaching high into the sky. This domain had once been the kingdom of giants, a race long gone. When Banion came to take over this castle, all that was found there was Morpheus, who proclaimed to have 'foreseen' Banion's coming. Theirs was a symbiotic relationship. Without Banion, the Warlock King's power was useless. Without the Warlock King, Banion was powerless to foresee and know how to overcome in this land.

The towers rose up some 150 feet from the ground behind a great wall, like stilts. Each tower was positioned as one part of a triangular design, so as to protect the castle from each direction; the south, the east and the west. To the north of the castle were the rocky crevasses and steep drops into the ocean. The rocky crevasses naturally formed a wall at the edge of the ocean serving to protect them from enemies at sea. Upon the top of each tower was a narrow walkway for guards to walk while on duty, much like a large widow's walk.

The guards that walked these posts were in charge of maintaining the catapults that were anchored on the wall of the tower. Three men worked each of these machines. Around the wall of the castle was a great moat, which was continuously fed with rushing water from the river that flowed out of the winter's mountain snow melt.

The Seltons, ancient relatives to the giants of old in this land, were trained military for Lord Banion. However, he showed no sympathies for the dwarves that had been captured in battles past. They became slaves and serviced the castles upkeep. The dwarves were hard working and lived very long lives, so once they were captured and their spirits were broken, they were compliant servants to their Lord. This came at great cost, for it was Morpheus who oversaw their 'training', making them subservient to their master. They worked as though in a trance, their home, a distant memory across the great ocean. Most dwarves had come to this land to discover new life. What they found was imprisonment and torture.

The moat was the habitat of monstrous reptile-like creatures. They were fed very poorly, keeping them hungry and ready to devour predators daring to intrude. From the two sides (east and west) of the castle, were drawbridges, used to cross over the dangerous moat. The intricacies of the drawbridge's mechanisms were dangerous to work on. Occasionally the pulley would get hung. A dwarf would then have to climb out onto it and adjust the pulley, freeing it from the trap. Climbing out on the pulley meant a possible misstep and the misfortunate dwarf would become supper for the hungry beasts below.

The front of the castle could not be breached. The wall ran for a mile from side to side before circling back around on either side to the ocean. Entering over one of the drawbridges was the only way to get in, unless you had a dragon; however, dragons were rare. In fact none was thought to be alive except Patarian. His story is for another time. But he came to serve Banion and bonded with him for life.

Guards were posted along the outside of the wall on each level, walking the distance of the wall ledge back and forth. Banion was always afraid of being attacked, although no one had attacked them in years. He had been successful with instilling fear throughout the land. Opposition had been subdued with the influence of Morpheus and Froc. But most importantly about this dwelling, deep within the bowels of this place, laid the much sought after treasure...the key to the locket, the key to peace.

Lord Banion was not born a 'lord' at all. In fact,

it was quite the contrary. He was born in the outer provinces of Duradane, the son of a smithy. His family was poor and Banion was in disfavor with his father; although, as far as Banion knew, it was for no particular reason. It was not uncommon for his father to come home having had a little too much ale and in a foul temperament.

When Banion was small, he would run to his father, full of life, excitement and anxious to share some piece of news of a new discovery, only to be dismissed by his father. There was never time for him or affection from his father. It wasn't long before Banion began avoiding his father. He would find a secluded tree to climb and spend hours dreaming and planning how he was going to escape from this horrible place.

The people from the province in which he and his family lived, despised his father, believing he had cheated them. They believed him to have lifted more money for himself than for King and country. The people would talk out loud, not trying to hide their hurtful words from Banion, when he was but a mere boy. People would talk about how crazy his father was. His mother would cower around Banion's father, because he had a reputation for having beaten her.

Banion was left to his own thoughts, often destructive ways, both to himself and to others. He grew consumed with hate and resentment. He had no friends and was bullied by other children.

Occasionally he would sit out on the fence post

of his home and see the King riding by with all his glory. Banion resented the King and all that he represented. It was at a very young age that he vowed to take revenge on all who never cared for him and those who he felt had destroyed his family. He needed a plan to be able to gain access to the King's castle. For this to happen, Banion would have to gain the King's trust. Banion did just that; he gaining the King's trust and allegiance. The King appointed Banion to his Court. As time went by, Banion became quite comfortable with his position. He became known as the Kingdom's Steward. This was quite a high position, as he was responsible for all of the wealth coming in and out of the castle.

One thing that the King forbade in his Kingdom was anything to do with the dark arts. While the King did befriend and take counsel with a White Wizard, Jarrod, this Wizard did not rule King Theymen's Kingdom. The King lived with an overwhelming faith in the power that came from above him. That power from above, ruled the King. He relied heavily on this faith to rule his people.

After a few years of service to the King, Banion began to dabble in the black arts. Witchcraft became an obsession. He found friendship with a warlock, whose name was Morpheus. The interesting part about this warlock was that Banion only saw him in his dreams. He spoke with him and they shared plans for overthrowing the Kingdom. Banion dreamt of

Morpheus, summoning a dragon...the dragon, later realized to be, Patarian.

Banion began to show his vengeful disposition, his evil thoughts and his dangerous mind. Since King Theyman had made a law against any kind of witchcraft, the King was forced to call judgment upon Banion. He was banished from Duradane, sentenced to a land called Swindalia, a place thought to have been deserted. Swindalia was in a different time and dimension. Banion would only be able to return if a lock and key could be found. Those items were enchanted and could not be found by anyone without remorse and goodness in their heart. Banion would have to search his heart to find those qualities. So Banion was cast out of Duradane by the White Wizard. His solitude made him even more bitter.

After roaming the desert land for days and weeks, Banion collapsed on the sandy ground. He would die and his dreams along with him. Banion fell to the ground, weakened, thirsty, hungry and ready to give up. Sleep came over him. In his sleep, he felt the coolness of water on his cracked dry lips and across the burned skin of his forehead. He saw familiar faces coming to his aid. *Was he dreaming? Was this renewed life after death?*

Banion opened his eyes, realizing he had been bathed, dressed and was lying on a soft bed. He had not been dreaming. Someone had rescued him from his demise. He turned his head to see that beside him sat a familiar face from his dreams. There beside him was Morpheus, the Warlock King, and beside Morpheus was Froc, the Black Wizard. With them beside him, Banion felt a new surge of energy, of conviction, of determination, and a desire to embrace the darkness.

Realizing that he was not alone, Banion believed that he could gain control of this land and the Seltons, the ancient tribe of Swindalia. Banion's protection and alliance with the Warlock King and with Wizard Froc created fear and submission of the people throughout the land.

As years followed, his power, greed and demented thinking made him go crazy. He had found his dragon, Patarian, during this time. Patarian had come from a larger flock of dragons which were thought to have been extinct or so deep in hiding that they were no threat to this Kingdom.

Pen It! Publications, LLC

Chapter 13

When Jade was taking flight from the Tree Elves' place of refuge, it was very early. Dawn had not yet shown itself. The air was cool. There was a quiet in these very early hours of the morning that was deafening. But Jade could feel the slight wind gusts brush under his wings gliding him upward without effort. Then as the gusts relaxed into a gentle breeze, Jade would fly, pushing his magnificent wings down and up defying the natural gravitational pull. Stars were still twinkling brightly, completely unaware of the events about to occur beneath them. As Jade was taking flight, he flew quietly, alone, looking back only briefly to the peaceful tree line growing smaller and smaller.

Jade rolled his head to face what lay before him. It was then that he heard the piercing screech of another dragon. It broke through the silence like a knife ripping time apart. Jade flew higher, so that he would not be seen, but he himself was at a disadvantage. He could not see this creature. Jade strained his eyes to see him, looking up, looking down, and looking from side to side. There was the screeching again, louder this time.

Pen It! Publications, LLC

Suddenly, with this last break in the quietness of the early morning, Jade was able to see where and who was beneath him. Further northwest of the Tree Elves home, where the base of the mountain met the desert's edge, Jade spied the other dragon, circling below him. His wings were royal blue with fiery red streaks racing through them. His shape was distinctively prehistoric, with horns extending from his head and spine down to the tip of his sharpened tail.

This must be Patarian.

While Jade knew that he was going to have to confront this opponent soon, today was not that day. *'I must find shelter,'* thought Jade. He flew higher, allowing the air currents to pull him up, trying to be as quiet as possible. *'The mountains,'* Jade thought. *'But where…where shall I go? I don't see a place to enter…there must be a cave entrance somewhere. Where?*

He continued to fly higher and toward the mountain's edge, abandoning the other dragon below. *'There! A ledge…and wait…'*

As his thoughts clouded with the fear of being seen, Jade strained his eyes to focus. *'Dare I trust my eyes? It looks like a cave.* His thoughts raced, searching for a plan as his eyes darted about searching for shelter.

He flew closer. It was a cave. Jade approached the ledge of the mountain with ease, landing gently and pulling his wings to his side. While this cave looked like a place to rest, there was no certainty that there weren't others who might be lurking inside. Cautiously, he approached the opening, its mouth wide and dark. He stepped in, hearing only the echoing of a steady dripping of water. Jade's eyes took a moment to adjust to the darkness. He moved slowly, positioning himself up on his hind legs ready to defend himself at any moment. He suddenly became aware of eyes watching him. He turned to look behind him, identifying the owners of those eyes: **Dragons**!

He was shouting in his mind. *Did he say that out loud? Did they hear his thoughts?*

The dragons in the cave met their eyes with Jade's eyes. Both were ready to pounce on the other.

One of the dragons spoke, "Who are you?"

Jade, equally uncertain of who he was talking with, only answered, "Jade."

"What are you doing here and how did you find this place?" the purple dragon said.

"He is an intruder!" another dragon insisted. "We must protect our family! We cannot trust that he is not another spy for Banion and that evil Patarian."

"Wait!" Jade said with conviction. "I am not a spy for Banion. I came here to hide from him and Patarian. He has been patrolling the area at the base of the mountain and the far side of the desert, along the tree line to the south of here. Who are you?"

"Yes," one of the dragons spoke up. "We have seen Patarian. We are the coastal dragons of this land. My name is Gabrieth. Many years ago we were forced into seclusion for survival. Banion came out of nowhere. He destroyed our land and enslaved those born in this country. He used deceit, lies, and the power from the Warlock King, along with the help from a Wizard, to overpower all who lived in this country. We are presumed to be extinct, as we have not allowed ourselves to roam any of the outside lands. No eyes have seen us for many years. Our numbers have grown and we have survived in spite of Banion. We have thrived and lived. We are still a strong force. But, we cannot win against such an evil power without help. We do not know what else lies out there in this land."

"I can answer some of your questions. Do you know that many other races have gone into hiding, much like you have done?" Jade began. He went on to share with Gabrieth and these cave dwelling dragons the long story of years gone by about the Tree Elves, Frederick and Jemma, his plan to overrun the Kingdom of Banion. The dragons listened intently. "Will you band together with us?" Jade asked.

"I do not know," said the leader, Gabrieth, still reluctant to let down his guard. "How can we help? Banion's black arts have driven us into seclusion and as long as they think us extinct, we will remain safe from our oppressors. I believe that we must take some time to counsel with each other. We need time," said Gabrieth.

"But time is our enemy, my friends," declared Jade.

"What do you mean?" asked one of the council

members in the crowd of dragons.

"I mean that unless we find the key to this locket," showing the locket around his neck, "we will not destroy any part of this evil in this land. I come from a land of a different time and place. I am here on what I would call, borrowed time. If I am unable to find the key within an unknown amount of time I may seal our fate and forever be here without the victory over this existing Kingdom, restoring your land. I plead with you for your help. You know these lands better than most. You have been here since the demise of your beautiful homeland. With numbers and knowledge we can defeat Banion. I believe that we each can do something. Perhaps all of us, together, can do it all; to rise up against Banion and his followers! We must create a diversion so that the two young children can get into the castle, find the key and then unlock the truth, dissolving this evil and setting right what was stolen from you and so many others. Please...you must help us," Jade pleaded.

Chapter 14

The children woke early full of apprehension. While the mood of this habitat was hopeful and optimistic, Frederick and Jemma were uneasy. Thoughts of home again invaded their minds and the unspoken words of the morning reflected in their eyes. Silent screams of fear and homesickness overwhelmed them, nearly paralyzing them from movement. What were they about to do? Would they wake up to find that all of this had been nothing but a nightmare? But then, how could both of them be dreaming the exact same thing? No, this was not a dream but the hard cold reality of what life had become.

It was still quite early when the birds had begun to sing, oblivious to any turmoil in the world except for whether Momma Robin could catch the worm. It was just before dawn, the air cool as the morning breeze slipped again through the open bedroom window, just as it had every morning since they had arrived here in this safe haven. Jemma and Frederick crawled out of bed, moving about the room gathering their things, dressing, and tidying up as they prepared for their journey. It was funny how peaceful it seemed this morning. What lay ahead was too much to grasp.

Pen It! Publications, LLC

Frederick stopped what he was doing and turned to face Jemma. He took hold of her arms, took a deep breath and said, "It's going to be okay, Jemm. We have help. We'll be ok," he said, then hugged her, as if this was all to help convince himself that there would be a happy ending to this journey.

There was a knock at the door.

"Yes?" they spoke in unison.

It was Toron. "Breakfast has been served. We leave within the hour. Please meet me in the courtyard."

Then Toron turned and left in silence without waiting for an answer. Toron was a rugged soldier and all about discipline and military tactics. However, in the few days that the children had been there, he had grown fond of the two humans. There was a sense of both loyalty and protection that he felt for them. He would do all that he could to protect them. After all, they did not yet know that their trusted companion had gone, and none of them knew where he was headed.

Without delay, the children finished their preparations for the journey. As they slipped out the door to head for breakfast, neither Frederick nor Jemma felt hungry. There was only a large, mixed up ball of emotions in their stomachs, leaving little room for any food. *Maybe some warm milk would help calm them. Maybe a few bites of oatmeal would do the trick.* They had no idea when they would eat again or what that meal might be. Nourishment now was critical.

Finishing their meal, they grabbed their belongings; satchels slung over an arm, and ran to the courtyard. Waiting there was a multitude of people: soldiers and military ranks standing waiting for their orders. Toron was there, talking with the King.

The King was dressed in full battle garb; armor that was shiny and smooth, clean and strong. He cradled in his arm his helmet, designed to protect his head and face. The armor was hewn by Elvin hands with care, fashioned and shaped to protect their King's life.

Suddenly the children's eyes scanned the perimeter looking for the one who was not there...Jade. *Where was he?* Surely he had come back from hunting or doing whatever dragons do to get ready for a battle.

"Toron!" yelled Jemma. "Where is Jade? Is he not back from hunting yet?"

Toron waved the children to him as he stood by the King. "Jemma, Frederick...Jade has gone on." The children gasped.

"What!" they both exclaimed.

"He feared that if he traveled with any of our regiments that he would be easily seen and jeopardize the mission. So, he set out very early this morning to look for another way to Banion and to avoid being a target for you two," Toron explained.

"But how will we continue by ourselves? We don't know the way! All of this is so much bigger than we are! Oh, Frederick!" Jemma began to cry.

"Children...oh, my children...I know that so much is expected of you, you who are so small, so young," began Toron. "But I am going with you. I will lead you around the desert. We will not march through, but we will hike toward the mountains. There we hope to find a river. This will be our road toward the castle. Close to the mountain range there is a line of trees that we can use for cover. You must trust me, as your friend and as your protector. I promised Jade that I would take care of you. My promise is my word. Nothing will harm you that I can prevent."

Just then a trumpet exploded into the quiet morning mist.

"Open the gate; it is one of our scouts. Let him in!" shouted the watch tower guard. The scout, Japheth, continued to run until he approached the King and only slowed to wait for his Highness's nod to come close. Out of breath, he knelt on one knee before King Ananon.

"My Liege, I bring you good tidings. Our military scouts have traveled to the land of the Grass Elves from the Eastern border. They came to meet us. They have agreed to work with us. They are gathering their armies to move up and flank the eastern side of the desert. They will approach the castle of Banion from there. They ask for reinforcements to aid them.

From their vantage point, they believe there is a secret valley that borders the desert allowing them to bypass the desert to reach the castle by the sea. They have been waiting to escape their hiding just as we have. When we told them about the two young humans, hope was renewed. For the last two days they have celebrated you, Master Frederick, Mistress Jemma. You will have a place in our history. I give you my allegiance," said Japheth.

"You have done well, Japheth. Are you well? Was it a long journey to the Grass Elves?" asked King Ananon.

"Yes," smiled Japheth. "I am well except for being a little hungry. But I will go where you call me to go and I will do what I am asked to do. All you need to do is say the word, my Lord," and Japheth's smile melted into a serious look of attention, devoted and true to his King. "It is about a four day walk to their settlement. I was able to do it in less than two days with my horse. I am ready to go back again if you so desire, my King."

"You rest and take nourishment," said the King. "You can leave tonight with reinforcements to aid the Grass clan. The rest of us are preparing to leave now. And Japheth," the King smiled and grabbed the young elf's arm, "please share my gratitude with their leaders. You will be well rewarded."

King Ananon then turned to the men still standing at attention. "It is time to leave. I will travel through the desert with my army, as that is what Banion would expect. Toron, take the children and lead them to the west toward the mountains. Perhaps there you will find the river that will carry you safely to the castle. May the one who watches over us all carry us safely through our task! May the people of Swindalia, fight as you have been trained. Bravely go forth with courage and righteousness on your side. Today is the day we have dreamt about for a century. Today is the day of our VICTORY!"

"Battalions! In your ranks," shouted the captain of the guard. "Open the gates! March, all of you, who count yourselves worthy of this honorable deed!"

The first group left, heading toward the mighty desert. Right behind them, Japheth lead another battalion, armed with their weapons of bows and arrows, knives, spears and rope, cutting back to the East to assist the Grass Elves.

Toron looked at Jemma and Frederick. "Are you both ready? Gather your things. Carry only what is necessary. We must leave on the heels of these two groups to slip out to the west as undetected as possible. Take courage, children. Life is full of trials but what does not break us will make us strong. Now get your things. Let's go."

Riddles for the Kingdom

Pen It! Publications, LLC

Chapter 15

Since the elvish people were so small, travel clothes fit the children well. The colors of their clothes were muted browns and greens and covered their arms and legs, camouflaging them as they journeyed. These clothes, enchanted by those who crafted them, took on the colors of the terrain, making it difficult to see them to an untrained eye. Nonetheless, it was important to travel with as much cover of forest as possible.

Toron led the way, slipping out of the protective seclusion of their tree houses toward the west, using the cover of the forest around them. In addition to the elfish rope, sword, spear, and knife that he carried, Toron and the children also carried a netted hammock to be used in the trees at night.

Finally, they carried a few utensils for preparing light meals and a meager supply of food rations for the road. The hope was that they could follow a northwesterly direction, enabling them to still use the trees to cover them at night. Sleeping in the trees had become a well-rehearsed practice for Toron and the trained soldiers under the realm of King Ananon. While this may have taken some getting used to by the children, Toron had confidence that they would adjust to their surroundings. And by the time they had hiked all day, just lying down and being able to close their eyes would be welcome.

The forest was dark and damp. Blankets of decaying leaves carpeted the floor. There was that moldy smell again, the one that the children had noticed in the cave below the river. Overhead were the eerie sounds of hoot owls talking to each other and perhaps sensing the danger in the air with a keen sense of awareness of something being "afoot".

One thing that Frederick or Jemma had not thought about was the danger from this natural habitat. *Were there bears or wild cats, wild hogs or buffalo?* Maybe there were animals here that they hadn't even heard about. At any rate, the threesome walked in silence while their thoughts ran rampant about possible danger.

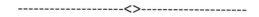

It had been several hours since they had set out and Toron saw that the children were tiring. "Do you need to take a break for a few minute? I have some small portions of food that may help strengthen you a bit. Sit, have a drink, and eat some of this," Toron held out slivers of what looked to be crackers or maybe a type of jerky.

"Thank you," the children said in unison.

"Where are we, Master Toron?" asked Frederick. "It is an odd place here. It reminds me of the forest that we escaped into after our home was destroyed. Only, I am sure glad you are with us, Toron. I wish Jade was with us too. Where do you suppose he is?"

"So many questions," said Toron. "We have crossed into the forest of Hanopolis, the city of trees. It is said that in this forest are Centaurs, but it was believed by my people that these creatures, like us, went into seclusion for safety. They are said to be very wise and good in battle. If we are so lucky to find these horsemen, I will try to convince them to help us. We are great in numbers if we have the Grass Elves and the Centaurs help. Now, enough chatter. We must press on. Are you ready Jemma and Frederick?"

It was late now and the canopy of trees made it look like night. As they stepped forward, Toron in the lead, they heard a rustling in the trees.

"What was that?" asked Jemma in a whisper.

All of them stopped, looked from side to side, in front and behind them.

"I don't really -------" began Toron.

Before either Jemma or Frederick could fully answer, there stood before them a tall horse-like creature with a man's head and chest, but the body of a horse. He began to speak.

"Halt! In the name of our Lord!" he demanded, as he held up his arm to stop them, tail swishing angrily behind him. "Who doth desire to pass this way? It is forbidden! Go forth from this place back to where you have come," said the beast.

For a moment, Toron and his companions stood there in amazement, frozen, mouths open, and thoughts racing concerning their safety. This creature looked serious and quite overpowering.

Toron seemed not to be afraid, but his size against this beast was intimidating. "I am Toron, of the Tree Elves. My King is Ananon. Our people are taking up with the Grass Elves on the eastern parameter to defeat the evil oppressor, Banion. Are you familiar with this man? These children have come here from a distant land. We believe they are the fulfillment of an ancient prophecy. It is through them that we will defeat this tyrant."

The Centaurs were not impressed, seemingly unfazed by the intruders' story. The Centaurs, being big, strong, and very powerful, had not, in these many years, been able to overcome Banion.

"We are quite knowledgeable of this man you refer to as Banion. It is a terrible thing what he has done to our people and our land. Many of our ancestors died trying to defeat him. But we could not survive against his dark arts used by his wizard and warlock king. We were forced into seclusion, but we guard this area carefully. Our people have repopulated in the quiet hidden Forest of Hanopolis. Those of us who have taken over the guardianship of our people guard this forest with our lives. How do we trust you? We trust NO ONE, especially Humans!" the leader of the group shouted.

Pen It! Publications, LLC

"I understand your fear...and I..." began Toron boldly.

"WE DO NOT FEAR YOU OR ANYTHING ELSE!" the large creature demanded.

Then there was a deafening silence for a moment while Toron gathered his thoughts to phrase his explanation differently and in a nonthreatening way. When the Centaurs beastly soul spoke, the earth shook. He was powerful and Toron knew better than to anger him to the point of using it.

"I beseech you, Lord. I do not mean to imply that you are not brave. Please forgive me this ill-phrased suggestion. Allow me to start again," said Toron, waiting for the acknowledgement to proceed.

"Go On!" the Centaur commanded, waiting for the justification for their intrusion.

"We, my people and I, believe that the prophecy of old, told to us about how Banion was going to be defeated, is coming to pass. We are living this history. Listen to the prophecy that you might understand our mission...not to impose on you but to ask for your help," said Toron. And he proceeded to articulate the beautiful riddle that his King had spoken just a few days before.

The lands of our fathers will be wrought with pain
and dismay
Your people will cry out for peace
but no one will hear.
The evil will progress and lives will be lost.

But upon this rock I will build a solid foundation, a hope,
a plan for justice and dominion over evil.

Two will come, though innocent and meek
They will be the key
as they face the evil in its dwelling place retrieving the truth for freedom.

Their strength will come from their friend,
A third to come,
One who will be powerful,
One who would not be tamed,
One with a driving force to be in this land.

You will know this sign by the locket they possess.
Your mighty armies will again be strong
And the lands and its peoples will come together as a mighty force.
Confidence will be restored and victory will belong to its true inhabitants.

"Have you ever heard this?" asked Toron.

"Who is this 'third to come' and where is this locket of which you speak?" the Centaur asked.

"The children brought with them a mighty dragon. He has gone ahead to make the path clear for the children. These children, Jemma and Frederick, of Duradane have found the locket which is being worn on the neck of this dragon. They must get into the castle to retrieve the key. It is through this that the spells will be broken and the power that Banion has over us will be lost. We could use your help. The task is great for these young humans but they have accepted the challenge. Will you not put away your hate and help us so that we can have our lives back, our people free to live in the land of our ancestors; that you may have your land back and roam the lands as your fathers did before you?" pleaded Toron.

"We will not help these humans!" protested the powerful creature. "But we will let you pass. However, do not presume to be able to come back through here. We would consider it an act of war against us."

The leader of the Centaurs threw his head to one side, as if to wave off his guards that stood with him. They stepped aside, making just barely enough room for the humans and the elf to pass. No one said another word.

Toron did not attempt to argue with the Centaur, but nodded his head at the beast and simply said, "Come along, children," passing the horsemen without a word or a look.

They walked with their heads down, only looking at the ground and their feet so as to not tempt any more interaction or wrath from the beasts. Once out of sight, Toron found a rock and sat down waiting for the children to join him. He was obviously rattled, perspiring and fidgety, rubbing his hands together and turning his head side to side, eyes darting as if trying to find something following them.

"What is it, Master Toron?" asked Frederick, not sure what to think...if they were in danger or free to move on.

"Children, the Centaurs are some of the most powerful creatures that there are in this land. If we cannot convince them to help us..." There was a silence by Toron that scared the children.

"What is it Toron?" Jemma pressed him for answers. "If the Centaurs don't help, then what?"

"In this country, the Centaurs are the most powerful ethnic group. Their strength and influence goes a long way in the success of us taking back our land. Why they do not want to engage with us is unclear, unless there is such a hatred for humans that they are committed to not aid your kind ever again," said Toron.

"Let us move on. We still have a mission to accomplish and sitting here pondering the whys of things will not get us to our destination or the job done. Can you walk a little longer? I would like to get beyond the proximity of the Centaurs. I am sure their scouts will follow us for several miles."

The threesome moved on, watching for any movement along the way. The few hours that they traveled seemed like an eternity. The air was heavy in this place and the stress of the unknown made them all weary.

When they could not go any farther, Toron, without saying a word, began to look up into the trees for a good place to camp. There was no shortage of good protection. He sat his things down on the ground and rummaged through his pack for a quick bite to eat for him and the children before beginning his climb into the trees. With his elvin rope, looped one end in one hand and holding the other end in his other hand, he set out to 'lasso' a tree limb, one that was high enough off of the ground to not be easily seen, one that would allow them to keep watch for unwelcome intruders.

Jemma and Frederick were too weary to do more than just watch. They were too tired for questions or any more discussion. So they watched and learned as the expert prepared for them a place to rest.

Toron spotted a tree not too far off their path that would work. As he held the looped rope in one hand, he began to swing the other end of the rope with the other hand until it was going fast enough to fly to its target, a very high branch in this tree. As the end of the rope caught hold of the limb, it snaked around it and tied itself securely. Toron tugged on it a few times to assure himself that the rope was snug.

"Okay, Jemma and Frederick," he began, "Come here and let me secure this around your waists," leaving room for himself in the front of the rope. "Make certain that any signs of us being here are removed so as to not give away that we are here."

The children were obedient, Jemma going first followed by Frederick. The rope had an interesting feel to it and even though Frederick really wanted to ask about it and how it was made, he thought better of doing so at this time. Toron then tied himself onto the rope in front of the children.

"Now, children, the rope will begin to pull us upward. Do not fight it but place your feet upon the trunk of the tree as we climb and walk with it as it pulls us. Hold onto the rope in front of you."

Then Toron began to speak to the rope in his native elfish tongue. "Boro levar omid lemgardium," Toron continued to chant as the rope began to move upward, the cargo in tow. Up they climbed, higher and higher into this giant.

Jemma turned to look at Frederick behind her and gasped at the distance from the ground that they had already come. This rope was moving and pulling them as if there was a person pulling on the other side of the rope.

"Jemma," Frederick said with a calm voice, "don't look down. Just keep your eyes on the back of Toron's head. It will be okay."

When at last they reached the selected area in which to conceal themselves, the rope began to magically encircle the tree weaving a platform on which they could work to secure their sleeping nets.

"Do not untie the rope from your waist until you are secure in your sleeping nets," Toron said as he stepped from the tree's trunk onto the rope carpeted platform. He then reached out his hand to guide Jemma onto the platform followed by Frederick.

"Whoa! Is this for real?" asked Frederick, his eyes wide with amazement.

"I assure you, lad, it is very real and that there is no stronger place to stand than this place," answered Toron. "Give me your sleeping nets and I will show you how to secure them."

He then began to attach them, one at a time throughout the branches of the tree. Then after helping the children to climb into the makeshift bed, Toron untied Jemma and Frederick from the rope to allow them to go to sleep.

"Now, grab hold of the other side of the net and pull it over top of you. It will shield you and blanket you for warmth," instructed Toron.

Without question or discussion, the children did as they were told and they were asleep in no time. While Toron wanted to get some sleep he remained alert and on watch for several hours of the night. It was only when he could bear it no more that his eyes drifted shut. He knew he would have to rest sometime in order to keep up his strength for the journey. Believing they were safely protected, he allowed himself to slip away into a semi-conscience sleep.

Frederick heard a small voice whispering, "Wake up. Get your sister up. We need to be going. Let me reattach the rope to your waist. We will climb down exactly the same way we came up. Here is a bit to eat," and Toron handed Frederick a parcel of food to chew with enough to share with Jemma. Both children were ready for their descent quickly.

Each day they delayed getting to the castle was a risk to the children not being able to return to their own home. Hours passed, then days, as they made their journey toward their destination. When the nights would come, the routine of how to climb the trees became easier and less scary. Food was available through berries found along the road or sometimes just forest bark that was edible. It was enough to keep their strength from dwindling.

On the 4th day of their journey, they began to see glimpses of snow- capped mountain peaks. The tree line was changing from tall oak and maple to birch, evergreens and fir trees, the ground under their feet covered with pine needles. When they first saw these glorious mountains, they unconsciously began to walk faster. But the elevation of the land was also changing, making their walk more of an uphill climb where the oxygen was thinner. It became increasingly more difficult to breathe and think clearly. Toron continued to push forward and eventually they found their way to the base of a steep mountain.

"How do we get up and over that, Toron? I can

hardly keep going now and my chest hurts. I'm having trouble breathing," Jemma said, voicing concern, not to complain but feeling the fatigue of their arduous journey.

"One step at a time, young lass. We do not have to climb all the way to the top. I believe that if my foresight has not gotten it wrong, there is a plateau that we can climb to then follow it to the intersection of the rivers flowing from the mountain top. It will be cold up there, however, and the river water will be running fast. We will climb this part of the mountain with the use of mountain hooks. See?" Toron said as he pulled out the Elvin rope and the hooks that he would need to scale the mountain.

"What is ... 'foresight'?" asked Jemma, turning and asking her brother.

"It's an elf thing, Jem. Don't worry about it," responded her brother. "Maybe he can see what happens to us now."

"No it is not clear to me, young lad. But perhaps our journey will reveal more as we go. Let us continue," Toron replied. "We will climb just like we climb the trees, scaling it with our feet firmly planted against the surface and hanging onto the rope. Only this time my job is a wee bit different. I will use these hooks by boring them into the mountain crevices and attaching this rope to it," he explained. "Jemma, you will be behind me as we do at night," Toron said as he attached the rope around her waist yet another time. "Frederick, are you okay with being my rear guard?"

"Oh, yes Sir!" replied Frederick with excitement. He had often spoken with his father about being a part of the Knights Realm, the closest guards to the King himself. This wasn't exactly that, but he felt important nonetheless.

They assumed their positions in line, allowing Toron to tie the rope and begin ascending against the steepness of the mountain. He carefully hammered each hook into the rock giving a foot hold on which the children to step. The tapping of the hooks into the hard surface took on a cadence...tap, tap, tap, click...tap, tap, tap, click...as Toron hammered the hook and then attached the rope into it.

But as strong and focused as Toron was, he found himself becoming weary at the task ahead. This mountain and the time to overcome it were not impossible, but it was overwhelming, even for him. However, Toron continued his work, not complaining or lending suspicion to the children that he was, himself, lacking strength. The children had nothing to do but step up and wait, step up and wait, step up and wait.

Stillness was all around them except for the faint whistle of the wind blowing across them...running to get past them and the mountain wall. Their thoughts wandered looking at the beautiful scenery. They had climbed high enough that they could see the tops of the trees. They looked more like furry clumps of green rather than trees. The surface of the ground below was beginning to look like a land map; the path which they had traveled had all but disappeared. The desert, once to the north, now lay to the east of them and the contrast between the land masses was unmistakable.

It was a clear day, the sky was cloudless and blue; the sun was bright and warm on their faces, but the air was becoming cooler the higher they climbed. The metal hooks became cold to touch and the air, its thinning oxygen, difficult to breath. They could smell the coolness like Christmas after a new fallen snow. They were feeling light headed and sleepy, much like they had when Jade had brought them to this land. But they could not risk slipping into sleep, lest they fall and pull their companions off the side of the mountain. How much longer they would have to climb no one knew; they only knew that they needed to keep going. The wind howled, singing its lonely, sad song.

"How are you doing, Master Toron?" shouted Frederick from below. He wondered how a person of such small stature could continue at this pace...there had been no ledges to rest and he was confident that Toron was tired, even though he was an adult.

Riddles for the Kingdom

Pen It! Publications, LLC

Chapter 16

*J*ade remained calm but confident in his attempt to convince these fellow dragons to aid in the defeat of Banion.

"I tell you the truth. This is a worthy effort. We ask that you join the Elves from the trees in the South, the Elves from the grass lands of the East and help us defeat this devil."

"Why should we help the Elf people? They despised us...they hate us!" responded Gabrieth. "These Elves have hated us since... since... since...forever. No one has ever told us why, but the rage between our two races has driven us apart even before we were driven into seclusion. Where were they when we needed them to protect us from the many deaths of our ancestors? Why should we help them?

"This is not just about helping the Elvin people," began Jade. "It is about restoring what is right from what is very wrong for all of us, Elves, humans, and dragons alike. We all have a place in this world, a purpose. Fight for your place in this world!

"You are a mighty dragon, Gabrieth. Your numbers are great and the bigger your population, the more room you will need to continue to live in a place suitable for your young families. Would you deny the opportunity for your sons and daughters to take back what is rightfully theirs, the land, the freedom to fly and hunt and roam these beautiful lands the way we are meant to do? How much mightier could you be? I am a foreigner here and I will not presume to have an answer to your interracial conflicts; however, you have much to gain by laying those feelings aside and coming together as one in purpose. Conquer Banion and his minions and TAKE BACK YOUR LANDS!"

The stillness in the cave became deafening. Moments passed without a word being spoken. Piercing eyes continued to bore into the intruding Jade. But what he had said was true, Gabrieth realized.

Gabrieth's thoughts raced. They had fought so many years to live in solitude. Being presumably 'extinct' was not easy for creatures of this size. If they went along with the Elves, they would, in a very short time, lose everything they had established over the past century.

"What about the Centaurs from the forest's edge? They still exist. At one time they were a strength, more mighty than the wind that holds our wings in flight. What do you know of them?" asked Gabrieth.

"I do not ...that is, I personally do not know anything about them. I was not aware that there were creatures like that," Jade answered.

"I assure you, Jade. They did exist at one time.

And while out hunting for food, my dragons have commented that they have seen them. They are out there hiding somewhere too. This is my proposal: Find the Centaurs. Convince them to join this alliance. Return with one of their arrows and we will join the alliance as well. Do you agree?" said Gabrieth.

"You ask much. I do not even know where to look. If I cannot convince you of joining, how might I convince them? Is there something that I can take them to show them that you still exist and that you are in this with us as long as they join us?" Jade asked.

Gabrieth pondered the thought for a few moments. If they sent something that had been burned by fire the Centaurs would accuse Jade of trickery, believing that he, himself, had tried to make it look like evidence of the dragon clans' existence. If they send a tooth, they would say that it belonged to Jade or that he found it, an archeological artifact. None of these things would convince them of their existence. There was but one thing that would prove to the Centaurs that they were alive.

"I must have a moment, Jade. I will return shortly," Gabrieth said.

As Gabrieth turned to walk away, the other dragons closed the circle around Jade. It had been their custom, should anyone find them that he would be put to death. They could not risk allowing the intruder to leave.

"I say we kill him!" shouted one of the dragons. No doubt his bark was at least as big as his bite. Jeers erupted from the den of dragons guarding their prisoner, agreeing that something needed to be done to silence this unwelcomed beast. They seemed pretty blood thirsty. After all, it was their nature to be wild, to hunt, to pounce on its prey. And they had become very proficient at surprise attacks in order to stay hidden from the outside world.

They began to chant, "Death to the Intruder! Death to the Intruder! Death to the Intrude!" All of them were snorting an occasional blast of fire in Jade's direction. The roar of the dragons' chant became louder and louder until Gabrieth returned holding something.

"ENOUGH!" Gabrieth ordered, obviously disturbed that his group of scouts had done their best to intimidate Jade.

Immediate silence filled the room.

"Jade, this is something that will surely convince the Centaurs of our existence. This is more precious than my own life, but I am willing to entrust you with its care. You must bring it back to me. This is the only way."

As Gabrieth said these words he walked closer to Jade and handed him an oval shaped object, blue and quite warm.

"This is my unborn child. When they see that the egg is nearly ready to hatch, they will believe you. They will know that we live. Perhaps this will help them to be persuaded to join in our allied effort to fight

Banion."

"I cannot!" whispered Jade, as he stared down at this beautiful treasure. "You need not sacrifice your own son. Your offspring is too precious; it's too great of a risk...surely there is another way...There is something else that..."

"No. There is not," Gabrieth interrupted. "Take him. Care for him. Keep him warm and return him to me along with the promise from the Centaurs."

"But Gabrieth!" interjected one of the other dragons. "I cannot believe that you are even considering this. We established our laws and restrictions for our protection! We cannot allow this intruder to leave here, let alone take your unborn! What are you thinking?" the angry crowd roared, spitting fire with their anger, ready to pounce on this foreigner when given the word.

"Enough!" roared Gabrieth.

It was rare for any of the dragons to cross their leader. He was the Alfa, earned by his dominance and proof of strength and wisdom. He had kept his race alive, prospering in the mountain caverns without notice, successfully isolating the dragon clans to the successful illusion of their breed's extinction. Silence was immediate, once again.

"Our clans have been robbed of our land and our freedoms much too long. I believed when we went into hiding so many years ago that one day we would have to come out, to fight, to fly and live in the light. How many of you have even known anything but this place? How many of your children have been born in this captivity? That is what this is, a prison! We are our own prisoners, because we have allowed a foreigner to dictate our world. This dragon, Jade, speaks of others who were pushed into captivity by fear! FEAR! We must stop this madness! You will join me; we will join Jade, if we can confirm others in a unified alliance. Now, Jade, take my future, my son. We are at a crossroads in our history. We must allow this. Step back," Gabrieth commanded of his guards. "Go, Jade. We will wait only three days before I send my legions after you. Do not doubt that if need be we will find you."

"What name have you prepared to give this unborn dragon?" asked Jade.

"He is to be called Zolon," whispered Gabrieth.

Jade looked deeply into the eyes of this master dragon. Tears were welling up in this father's eyes. A father sacrificing his only son, risking his own very existence...this was a familiar story but very rarely seen in these days. His love must be greater than the love for life itself.

Jade took the frail treasure and tucked it under his wing, holding it securely until he could get to his destination.

"Where do I go to find these Centaurs?"

"You must fly south above the mountain until you see the edge of the trees. This is the Forest of Hanopolis. I believe the western side of the forest will provide what you are looking for. Go there. They will find you," instructed one of the dragon scouts.

As Jade walked to the edge of the cave and looked out into the wild, the still before the storm, feeling the cool breeze of the mountain against his chest he turned to take one last look at these beasts of his own kind…but they were gone. Had he just dreamed what he had just seen and heard? Was he just hoping to find others of his kind so badly that he became delusional? And then he reached under his wing with his talon and found the precious commodity which he possessed. This was no dream. The fight was about to begin.

Riddles for the Kingdom

Pen It! Publications, LLC

Chapter 17

*T*oron was tired. His training prepared him well as a soldier, but there was no real test for being ready except by being part of the battle. Climbing a ragged-edged mountain was a lot different than climbing trees.

"Just a little farther, young warriors," encouraged Toron. He began to chant the warriors cry, *"We march, march, march to victory, every man strong and fierce. From the treetops of Lambardeny to the castles of our enemies. We will fight; we will win; we will take our victory in."* With each phrase, Toron would drive another pin into the wall, the rhythm of the chant giving them all energy and renewed purpose. Their pace was quickened and time began to pass faster. The children began to focus on Toron's chant and joined with him in the soldier's war cry.

We march, march, march to victory.
Every man strong and fierce.
From the treetops of Lambardeny,
To the castles of our enemies.
We will fight, we will win,
We will take our victory in!

Before they knew it, they were climbing up onto a precipice, pulling themselves onto the level edge, hands and knees falling forward on the stone ground. They had arrived. Another leg of the journey was behind them. They had reached the mountain top.

"Everyone alright?" asked Toron, a little winded but with a slight grin on his face and an air of arrogance at their accomplishment.

Both children were too tired to speak but their eyes said everything. They were soldiers! They had followed their captain and made it to the top. Their eyes smiled as their mouths hung open gasping for that precious oxygen.

"We will rest here for the night, but we need to find an area where we cannot be spotted. I am not sure what is here, in the sky or on land," said Toron.

Once they had recovered from being out of breath, they picked themselves up and began to walk. Who would have thought that walking would be so easy; but after the climb they had just made, they had new perspective.

Toron, Jemma and Frederick hiked until they came to some brush that would hide them for the night. Again, Toron pulled out the Elvin bread to sooth the empty stomach.

"I feel like my throat has been cut; I'm so hungry!" said Frederick taking the bread from Toron without hesitation or complaint.

"I know this isn't much, but it will have to do.

We will rest for just a short while and continue. We must try to figure out how to get from here to the castle. I do believe it is not far," said Toron.

"Then how do we get into the castle?" asked Jemma.

"One step at a time, my girl; one step at a time," Toron answered as the conversation faded.

It was dusk when they lay down. Night fell quickly on this day, at the very top of the world. As they lay on the ground, looking up at the sky, they all marveled at its beauty. The stars glistened like diamonds, some of them darting across the dark canvas with tails that stretched behind, chasing their leader into oblivion. As he propped himself against a nearby bolder to keep watch, Toron reached his finger out to the sky simulating an act of touching the star.

This was a game he liked to play when he was a child, dreaming of adventure and other worlds. The quiet peacefulness of the vision brought with it heavy eyelids to all three of them. In spite of their anxiety about what lay ahead, all of them were exhausted. Sleep swept over them. Toron tried to stay awake, but even he succumbed to the physical fatigue from the journey. Their dreams were unsettled, vivid and mysterious. They all knew that they were approaching the dreaded destiny, Banion's castle.

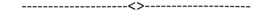

When Toron awoke, it was still dark. He raised his head from his chest and looked around his surroundings. He gathered his thoughts and got up to go wake the children.

"Jemma," he shook her gently.

"Frederick," he whispered, and shook him, as well.

"We must move on. It will be safer to travel when it is dark," whispered Toron. "Put some of this on your face and hands." He handed them some brown paste that he had made from mud and water. "Hopefully this will help camouflage us while we are out in the open."

"Hey!" Frederick stopped abruptly to listen. "Do you hear that?"

"It is the river that flows from the mountain down to the sea," said Toron. "This may be our way down to the castle. As the snow on the mountain top melts, the water rushes to the bottom of the mountain creating quite the collection of rapids. I'm not sure how we will get down. Perhaps scaling the other side like we did coming up?"

They continued walking toward the sound, careful to stay as camouflaged as possible. When they first spotted the water, it appeared to be a swirling pool that moved as a slow current to the larger sound. Toron approached the water's edge, looking at his own face staring back at him in the water.

"Where do we go from here, great leader?"

Toron thought to himself mockingly as he stared at his reflection.

"How do we get down the mountain Toron?" asked Jemma.

As Jemma waited for Toron to answer, Frederick continued to look around the pool. He looked down into the water and began to see an image that was not his own. It beckoned him as he became transfixed on the image.

The image spoke. "Go down the river. Seek what you yearn for in the bowels of the evil dwelling. BEWARE! Do not tarry!"

The image left with only a ripple in the water and Frederick's reflection staring back. He snapped out of the trance-like state like he was being shaken from a dream. He had seen this image, this face before. He knew who it was.

"I know what to do!" Frederick shouted. "I know what to do! Toron! Jemma! We have to get down the river to the castle, to the dungeon! I saw the White Wizard in a vision, just now! It was him and he told me that is what we have to do!" Frederick looked frantically for a boat or something to carry them.

No boat was found, so they continued walking, their pace increasing with the excitement of being so close. Fear was replaced momentarily with resolve to just get down that mountain. One way or another, they were going to do it.

They spotted a small vessel almost at the same time. It was a canoe, made of dark gopher wood, short from end to end but carved deep inside for its passengers to sit securely or row while on their knees. There was a long piece of wood, one toward the front of the canoe end and one toward the back that stretched perpendicularly across either side of the canoe and over the water for balance. It was obvious that this was built for rougher waters. Tied to a bush, it beckoned them. It was as though someone put it there for them.

Without hesitation, they jumped in, each grabbing a paddle that had been left inside the vessel, and each eager to ride...first Jemma, then Frederick and last, Toron who untied the rope that had been securing the boat. Pushing off into the watery path, Toron jumped into the boat. Dawn was breaking. As they moved quickly into the river's current, they began to see the fierceness of what they had gotten themselves into but there was no turning back.

The water raged. Rapids became bigger and more violent, the water slamming up against the boat from all angles, against the misplaced rocks in their path and splashing the flying water into the boat. As the rapids continued to crash upon each other, they slapped the boat, pushing it from side to side as it increased its speed going down the side of the mountain. Toron used his paddle as a rudder, trying to steer the boat into the safest part of the path but it was too powerful to control. All they could do was ride it out.

Suddenly there was a calm in the water. The river was still pushing them but the river opened up just enough for the water to pool without rapids. There is a saying about the "calm before the storm." This was it. As the three passengers began to relax from their fierce ride, they looked ahead at the sound of a roaring monster. Ahead of them it looked like the river just ended, like it dropped off into the end of the world.

Toron realized his worst fear yet. The river had led them to a waterfall. As they drifted to the edge of its grasp, Toron yelled, "GET DOWN IN THE BOAT! HANG ON!"

He had barely spoken when the boat slipped over the edge and fell until it crashed to the bottom, dipped under the water and punched back up through to the surface. Amazingly, all of them were still in the boat. Toron was quickly back up on the rear of the boat, shouting out instructions. The rapids were trying to eat them alive. The water roared.

"We have to be able to get the boat stopped before we get washed into the mote! We won't survive the crocs. The water is running so high that I fear we'll not be able to get stopped by the gate," Toron shouted. "Quickly Frederick, Jemma...PULL!"

The children pushed the ends of their paddles into the water beside the boat and pulled as hard as they could while Toron continued to try to steer the boat and shout out his quick paced instructions, "PULL...PULL...PULL...PULL!"

Still using his paddle as the rudder, Toron was

pulling hard left, directing the boat to the edge of the river. As they rolled through the white water, its fury crashing over the bow of the boat, the left side of the boat hit a 'hole', a place where the rushing water fell over a rock and doubled back over itself creating a sucking vortex; the boat was getting sucked into the water's jaws. The boat flipped, throwing all of them into the rushing rapids. Arms, legs and paddles were flying awry, flailing about, and sucking the children under with the undertow current. Turning and tossing under the water separated Toron from them but he was flipped toward the bank and was able to grab a paddle along with the arm of someone. He pulled himself, paddle in one hand and child's arm in another hand up onto the bank of the river.

"Jemma! KICK GIRL! KICK!" Using all of his strength, Toron pulled her onto the bank with him while surveying his surroundings for Frederick. "Frederick! Frederick!" he shouted.

"Look, Toron. On the rock! Up river! He's alive! He is hanging on the rock!" shouted Jemma.

Toron looked up the river, searching for the boy. When at last he saw him, Frederick was hunched over a rock, feet still dangling in the water.

"Frederick! Are you okay? Frederick!" yelled Toron.

It was so loud, the water rumbling and roaring like a large monster threatening to consume those who would chance saving this boy. Suddenly Frederick raised his head, coughing and spattering water. As he looked around, he saw Toron and Jemma. There was water gushing between the rock and the river's edge where they stood. Frederick pulled himself upon the rock he was holding and into a stance, waiting for Toron to tell him what to do.

"Frederick, can you hear me?" shouted Toron. The young boy gave a nervous nod, eyes wide and scared. "I am going to throw you the rope! Tie it around your waist! Tie it snuggly! Tie it the way we tied it to go up the trees at night! Remember? Can you do that, my man?" shouted Toron.

Toron took the elven rope and tossed one end of it across the water to the rock. The first time it did not work and the rope nearly fell into the water.

"Try again, Toron! I can't reach it! Throw it farther!" Frederick screamed his voice shaking and impatient.

Toron tried again and again. Jemma stood back shivering, partially from the cold water and partially from her stone cold fear. Teeth chattering, she sat down behind Toron in a fetal position and waited, prayed, and hoped.

Once again Toron threw the rope; this time with so much momentum he nearly threw himself with the rope back into the water. Jemma reached up to grab Toron's ankle to keep him from falling back into the stormy river.

"If I can get him close enough with the rope, I can pull him in with the paddle."

With one more heave, the rope end reached the rock, not quite to Frederick. The boy crouched down on the rock onto all fours and inched his fingers toward the rope end. The water behind the rock was slamming into it so hard he could feel the rock being pushed. One good wave and it could push him over the edge without the rope.

"One more inch...almost got it... there!" Frederick mumbled to himself. "GOT IT!" shouted Frederick. "I have it!" he yelled.

"Tie it around your waist!" Toron yelled.

Obediently Frederick sat back on his knees and tied the Elvin rope around himself. "You haven't failed me yet! Don't fail me now!" Frederick muttered.

As Toron watched the boy do what he was told, he shouted the next instruction. "Now jump into the water! Feet First! Keep your toes up and stay on your back! Feet first down river!"

"What? You want me to jump in? I can't! I just can't! I'm too afraid!" and for the first time, Frederick began to cry.

Jemma stood up so he could see her. "Frederick, it will be okay! Do what he says. It is okay; you are okay!" Jemma encouraged.

"Jemma's voice...yes...Jemma was okay..." thought Frederick. Her voice was the reassurance that he needed. "I can do this for you, Jemm! I will do this for US!"

He jumped into the frothy jaws of the watery

monster and felt the rope tighten so snugly it felt like it was squeezing the life out of him. That rope had a mind of its own and it was not going to let go. Was he being pulled or pushed? As he went through the rapids, riding the ups and downs of the running water, he forgot that when he rode up on the wave he should grab a breath. It was backwards. He was trying to breathe when he went under...sputtering and spitting when it pushed him up. Toron pulled the rope, hand over hand...pulling, pulling, and pulling until Frederick was close enough to reach the paddle. He lowered the paddle down to him.

"Frederick! Take hold! Take hold of the paddle!" demanded Toron.

As the boy rose up on top of the water he saw the paddle and grabbed it with both hands. Toron pulled him to where he could grab his arms and pulled him up the bank of the river to its edge...finally safe, exhausted, wet, cold, and coughing up the water from his burning lungs.

Riddles for the Kingdom

Pen It! Publications, LLC

Chapter 18

*A*s Jade fell off of the edge of the cliff's steep precipice, allowing the air under his wings to catch him, he soared smoothly away from this shelter. He spoke to the unborn dragon he held, his thoughts and fears erupting into the silent air around him.

"You do not know of life, yet you are asked to do a task that may save your people; that may set your people free. I fear for all of us. How do we fight against an evil so big? You are so little, not even grown big enough to be born. I promise you, I will do all that is within me to protect you." Jade looked down and grasped the small object slightly tighter, as though he was offering a hug.

Jade flew for many hours, his wing span allowed him to glide for long distances while saving his strength for an unknown distance on this journey. He thought of Jemma and Frederick, wondering where they might be just now. *Had they found the mountain? Were they safe?* Without them, the journey would be for nothing.

He found himself thinking of the young man in the cave laying and waiting. *Would they get back to him? Why was he so familiar?* The feeling of protection he had toward this unbroken egg was what he had felt when looking upon the face of this man in the cave. Hope was what he had to hold on to and he knew it. As he flew further southwest, he began to spot the green of the forest. From the sky one could see the beauty of this treasured land. It seemed to give him energy and excitement.

"Okay, Centaurs. Do you see me coming? Where are you? Show yourselves."

From where he flew he could see the road that was no more than a walking path along the edge of the forest. Rather than land right away, he chose to circle from above. He made large loop-to-loops around this end of the forest hoping to attract its keepers. As he looked down, he thought he spotted a horse running between the trees.

"There! Young Dragon! I see him. We will follow him."

His keen eyes followed the dance of the beautiful creature's run. Jade looked beyond to a clearing where, standing in the thicket, were a large herd of these horse/man creatures. They had seen him, alright. The dragon continued to circle them and spiral downward closer to them. They were looking at him as if they had never seen his kind before. Fear was prominent in their watchful eyes. They listened, tails swishing, ears laid back and then flicking back to attention to hear. They could hear Jade's beating wings against the air until it was no more. Jade had landed.

Silence fell between them, the two species of

life that had never seen the other. *Was it fear or just amazement?* Like being snapped out of a trance, one of the Centaurs stepped forward to confront the other beast.

The Centaur was adorned with necklaces and bracelets and wore feathers in his hair. His skin was bronze, his chest strong and muscular, his hair dark, falling into long ringlets around his face and head. His chin jutted forward and he appeared to have a rather large nose as well as very big brown eyes with beading tattooed above the eyes. As he began to speak to the dragon, his voice was loud and deep. He was no doubt the one to whom others answered. His body was, of course, that of the equestrian family, his fur also dark with a very long and thick swishing tail. His legs were strong but thin and his feet or hooves were large with tufts of fur around his ankle area. No doubt he could cover a great deal of territory in a very short time when situations demanded it.

"Who...what...," began the Centaur, unable to formulate his question as he beheld the animal before him.

Jade interjected. "My name is Jade. I have traveled here from a distant land and-----"

The Centaur did not listen but tried again to formulate his question. "What are you? You are not from here. What do you want?"

"I am a dragon, my lord. I am one of many in this land. However, while I have come from a distant land, the dragons of Swindalia have been-----"

"Extinct!" shouted an elder Centaur in the crowd. "They have not existed here since the evil master took over so long ago. I have never seen a dragon! How magnificent! Can you breathe fire? How have you come to be? Your kind is extinct! We believed you to be no more!"

Jade, trying to be patient so as not to insight fear or a battle, began again. "My name is Jade. I am a dragon. The pod of dragons of which you speak, from your land, is not my family. However, I come to you today, to give witness to our breed's existence. The Dragons of Swindalia are not extinct, nor have they ever been. Like you---"

"Liar! They have been extinct since before my grandfather was born!" erupted one of the Centaurs in the crowd.

Silence grew between them, as tension mounted. Jade labored not knowing how to proceed. "Take me to your leader please. Allow me to explain. There is much for you to know and understand."

The beasts' eyes were darting up, down and around looking for more of these creatures like the one before them, fearing a trap. They had become untrusting, nervous creatures and felt threatened in their isolation. The sky remained unchanged; blue with white puffy clouds, but no more dragons.

"You may speak to me," announced the large Centaur with big brown eyes.

"I come to enlist your help. The true owners of

these lands are coming together to take back their rightful place. The Elves from the south, the Elves from the east, you, if you will join with us, and -----," Jade rolled his hand out holding the tiny treasure with his talons, "the Dragons from the West. Here is proof of their existence. This is the unborn child of the Dragon leader, Gabrieth. I present this egg as proof of their survival in Swindalia. Gabrieth has agreed to help in our efforts to defeat Banion if your people will join with us. Will you help?"

The man-beast moved closer to Jade, not taking his eyes off of the egg. "Allow me to hold this and examine it," said the Centaur.

Jade gently passed the small object to the Centaur. He stroked the soft warm shell with his hand in disbelief.

"You say this is an unborn dragon? How can I be sure?" asked the Centaur. "I have never seen a dragon's egg. It could as likely be some other kind of fowl or animal, a trick to lure us out from our hiding."

"I will not risk this youngling's life by aborting him before he is ready to be born. His father's hope is that he will be born into a free Swindalia. Who else could bring to you another dragon's egg but a dragon like me?" continued Jade. "But to free Swindalia we must unite and take it back from the evil Banion. If you join us, Gabrieth agreed to come out of hiding too. Please. I plead with you. Join with us."

As Jade spoke, his emotions pushing his voice louder with emphasis on his plea, the Centaur remained stoic, staring with icy, untrusting eyes. Silence fell on them again.

"Well?" Jade said, the silence becoming uncomfortable.

Suddenly the Centaur handed the egg back to Jade and stepped back. "I will declare to you as I did to the three who passed here several days ago. We will have no part in this war."

"Three?" Jade repeated the word. "Who are the three you speak of?"

"Two children and one elf. They had the same story. We allowed them to pass with the promise to not return. Our scouts followed them to the edge of the mountain."

"I plead with you," Jade begged. "Please join us!"

"We will not. Your time here is over. You will take your leave," the Centaur demanded.

Jade knew his efforts were exhausted. The group of Centaurs positioned themselves with arrows ready to fire directly at Jade, the sound of the bows drawn with such precision that it sounded like an army called to attention. He backed away slowly, tucking the small oval shell under his wing in protection. Not waiting, Jade took flight. When he was far enough away, he turned and flew straight up and out of the meeting. He flew hard and fast for the biggest part of an hour before he allowed himself to glide.

His mind raced, thinking about the confirmation

of the children's travels, and that the Centaurs wouldn't help. Now how was he going to convince Gabrieth to help? Their home, their cave, their structure of isolation had become no more than shackles.

He would have to figure out how he was going to win over the dragons since the Centaurs had obviously refused to take part in the battle ahead. Jade flew hard to reach the cave's entrance.

It was dark when he arrived at the mouth of this hidden space. He walked carefully into the hollow mouth of the mountain. Torches were lit not too far in but far enough back so as not to show light to the outside of the cave. Darkness flooded outside the cave entrance so one could see if there was the slightest spark of light. As Jade continued into the hollow space, no one seemed to be around. "Where are they, little fella?" Jade whispered to the young unborn dragon. "Hello?" Jade spoke hesitantly. "Is anyone here?" Jade continued walking deeper into the cave. It seemed odd that after he was so abruptly met the first time he came into this cave that there would be no one guarding the entrance on this night. As Jade turned a corner in the cave leading into a deeper tunnel, one dragon came to his call.

"You carry our leader's child. You must be the dragon known as Jade."

"I am. Where is everyone? Why are there not guards posted at the front?" asked Jade.

"They are all gone," answered the dragon

greeting Jade.

"What? Gone? What do you mean gone? Gone where? Who all went? Is there anyone in charge here?" Jade spoke without waiting for answers, frantic at the unknown.

"I do not know. What I do know is that there was trouble at the river, at the bottom of the river, near the place where Banion is said to live. Our scouts reported needing help. Those trained in combat left with Gabrieth. That's all I know. We who are in training for combat were left to take care of our families. Come in and have something to eat. It is not safe to venture out more tonight," said the young soldier.

Jade sighed with bewilderment and anxiety. His thoughts raced to Jemma and Frederick. *What if they were in trouble?* He knew he wouldn't sleep, but he was tired from his journey to and from the forest of Hanopolis. Maybe the others would return yet tonight with news of having seen and helped Jemma and Frederick. This night would prove a challenge, time lingering with only more unanswered questions.

Chapter 19

$\mathcal{W}$ ith one of King Ananon's most trusted commanders guiding the human children to the castle from the western edge of the desert and over the treacherous mountains, the King took it upon himself to lead his Cavalry from their gates of safety. It was more customary for the King to remain in the back of the regiment rather than lead from the front. But King Ananon would not lend himself to do this act, as he saw it as an act of fear to his people. His mission was to lead two battalions to the edge of the desert, divide his men, with one group going on through the desert and the other group going on to meet with his scout and the Grass Elves to the East.

As a young prince, the King remembered riding out along the desert border's edge and as far East as he deemed 'safe'. But as a young, inexperienced boy, he was often over-confident and thought himself invincible. He would risk his life and his companion's life going into ill-advised areas. So King Ananon did have some knowledge of the lands. He had faithfully done the same to the west even so far as to be spotted by a Centaur who chased him out of the forbidden Hanopolis forest. As his father and mentor would share the stories of the forgotten time before Banion, the young prince, filled with excitement for adventure, would ponder on how many of these other creatures still existed. He had seen the Centaur.

What about dragons? No, they were, if ever in existence, now extinct. He had ridden into a camp of Grass Elves once. They were none too thrilled. As he grew into a man, he set his sights on uniting others with his people. When he heard the legend, he believed that under his rule that this freedom and the unity of this world's existence would come. He lived with the hope and belief that the different species would join together. In the book of life that had been passed down for generations, there was a verse that was engraved and hung on his wall in the palace.

"The lion will lie down with the Lamb and Nations will come together united for one purpose...Peace."

These things continued through King Ananon's mind as his group traveled closer to the point of splitting up. Travel was difficult. As armies marched from the trees to the clearing just before the desert's edge, the ground was uneven and grass was thick, tall, dry and dying. Brush and thorn bushes were thick and difficult to miss while marching over the terrain. For the average human adult, this would have been difficult but for the elf, whose stature was smaller, the height of the grass, weeds and thistles was extremely challenging in which to maneuver. Nonetheless, they continued the march until finally reaching the desert, an abrupt change from the overgrown weeds to the very hot sand. As King Ananon stood at this precipice, he looked ahead; miles and miles of sand with no sign of water or sustenance. It was overwhelming.

"Japheth! Get the men in their ranks. I want to talk to them before we separate," said the King.

"Yes, Sire," Japheth said, lowering his head and backing away from the king.

King Ananon continued taking in the surroundings in front of him. It amazed him that there would be such an abrupt change from beautiful flowing trees to overgrown grass and weeds to the sparseness of any life; just a few rocky boulders and cacti around the pale brown sand. He had forgotten what a diverse country it was that they lived in.

The sun was pressing down upon him. This sand was hot, and would get into every crease and fold of clothing or skin exposed. And then there were the boots; getting sand into the boots was horribly uncomfortable. Walking too long with it between your feet and the bottom of the inside of your boot would, in a very short time, create large blisters on your feet. Sore feet were a bad beginning for soldiers going into battle. Each soldier would carry with him a substance called Epsom Salts, which soothed and helped to heal the woes of the feet. Soaking the feet in the warm water laced with this stuff took away the soreness.

Few had the opportunity to use this luxury as they marched toward battle. King Ananon turned to face his armies as he heard them snap to attention, the sound echoing across the ranks. He wanted for each one to see him, to hear his call to arms, to be encouraged by his voice of confidence.

"We ARE the mighty Elves of the Trees. We are the keepers of the land and redeemers of Freedom," began the King. "We embark on the next steps of our journey. Here is where some of us will depart. As we have trained in preparation, so we will fight: fierce, brave, and ready to take our Victory!"

Applause erupted, as King Ananon paused to allow his men to become excited.

"I honor you today; from the most highly ranked to the lowest, for all are significant in purpose. I bow before you and ask a blessing, from the most highly ranked to those who fight in the trenches of the battle, in the fiercest war zones, for success in mission. There will be a day to lay down arms and enjoy the fruits of our labor, but today is not that day! Today, we fight to regain what is ours and what belongs to many who, like us, have been in hiding for these many years. So now, I commission you to go forth into the desert or to the Grass Elves, our distant relatives, and conquer our enemies. Fear not, our Maker says, for I AM with you! Believe in this promise and rest in your conviction! When we meet again, we meet in VICTORY!"

The troops erupted in loud shouts, elated excitement and support. Today, history was going to change.

"Lieutenant! Call your troop. We will march on. Good travels my friend," the King said to the officer.

From the back of the company came an unfamiliar shout to the King. "My Liege!"

Ananon looked up stretching his neck to and fro to see who it was that had addressed him.

"Look, my Lord, over there!" exclaimed Japheth. Japheth stretched out his arm pointing his finger at the large beast now walking to the front of the line toward the King. Immediately the soldiers began to raise their weapons to protect their king. This creature had never been seen before by any, save one, the King. Mouths dropped in awe of this fantastic beast who was addressing their King.

"Let him pass!" ordered the King.

The Centaur continued his procession to the front, toward the King. As he approached him, Ananon's thoughts reflected again on when he was a young boy when he had run into these great creatures. He had forgotten how big and magnificent they were. The beast bowed his head in respect as he approached the King. Ananon mirrored the action.

"My name is Demetrius. I am the leader of the great herd of Centaurs in this land. We have remained isolated, chained to the circumstances of our imprisonment. For too long our leaders have denied that life can exist outside of our forest walls. But I am here to tell you that as occupiers of this land we desire to take back what once was ours. After having been seen by others who now know of our existence and place of refuge, we have decided to fight. If we die, we die honorably and for the good of all. Twice our leader has denied would-be allies the help needed to overtake Banion, to see the world as it was meant to be seen in all of its beauty and with all of its creatures that share in the responsibility of the land. So today, I, Demetrius, declare the Centaurs to be allies with the Elves, the Dragons and all of those other creatures who aspire to right what was wrong, my Liege. How may we help?"

Cheering again erupted with applause and exhilaration. The King approached the giant reaching up to embrace this new stranger as his friend. "Welcome, Comrade!"

They spoke a short time while making the plan to include the Centaurs. "We have three large herds with us. Perhaps one of our herds can go with the group of Tree Elves across the desert. The other group of us can accompany you to the Grass Elves to aid their attack from the right flank. Have you spoken to them?" asked Demetrius. "We can also be a back up to your battalion as a second unit to attack through the desert; to clean up what was missed the first attack."

"I have not laid eyes on this group of Grass Elves since I was a child. However, my scout has spoken with them. They agreed to help and their plan was to attack from the right side of the castle. I just don't know how to safely get them there without being noticed. They, like us, are short in stature making their marching long and hazardous. You could get to the castle faster but you would be unable to scale the walls," said King Ananon.

"I have an idea. Let us depart immediately so that I may present it to the Elves of the Grass, for it will take a joint effort for it to work," said Demetrius.

No time was wasted. The companies were dispersed, one going with a herd of Centaurs to the desert, one group of Centaurs with the King toward the Grass Elves and a group of Centaurs to stand back to wait a half day more to advance across the desert from the forest.

Chapter 20

*N*ight was falling. The stars shone brightly overhead. But something was amiss in this usually quiet setting. From the Grass Elves' home, there came a sound of thunder like they had never heard before. There was a hush among them. This thunderous noise was from the ground, not from the sky where it was usually detected. Or was it thunder? Fear seemed to spread through the people of this clan. From the watch tower of their dwelling, even the tower itself began to shake.

The tower watchman shouted, "Fighting positions! This is not thunder! Fighting positions! Captain of the guard, prepare your armies!"

From the tower the watchman could see the Centaurs driving toward them. There was no offer to stop or to draw arms to fire on the Elves. But as they rode closer, the watchman also saw the other smaller forces coming up behind them. He saw it was the Tree Elves.

In astonishment he screamed, "HOLD YOUR FIRE! FRIEND, NOT FOE! HOLD YOUR FIRE!"

On the back of the leading Centaur was an Elf. King Ananon had mounted Demetrius and driven the forces toward the Grass Elves. As they approached, the

King held up his hand in peace to halt the stampede of forces behind him.

"Watchmen!" the King called out. "We are here to help take back our lands; to drive the forces of evil from this place; a place that was once EDEN! Are you with us? I say, ARE YOU WITH US?!"

From the base of the tower, another unfamiliar character walked out to approach King Ananon. The King slid off of the back of Demetrius.

While there was room to ride on the back of the Centaurs, this was not natural for either of them, the Centaurs or the Elves. The Elves very obviously preferred to keep their feet on the ground. But this would get the elves in position in a much timelier manner so that they could scale the castle wall and bring down Banion and his soldiers.

"Who am I addressing?" asked King Ananon.

"I am Solomon, seer over the Grass Elf Clan. Our forces are armed and ready to leave. We cannot ride. We do not know how. We will march, as we always have into battle."

"I do understand, sir. We who are of the trees have never ridden either. But, this will allow the wonderful element of surprise. Banion will never see us coming. The Centaurs can get you to the wall and leave you to climb it from right flank and behind, seaside. With the Centaurs there we will have the place surrounded. The other beauty of this plan is that Centaurs are intelligent, strong warriors, creatures who even in their isolation have learned to fight. You don't have to do anything but ride. They have the burden of getting you there. I submit to you that this is very unorthodox, but this was their idea and it can work! I know that it can!" said Ananon.

The small Elf raised one eyebrow, as he was thinking about what the King had said before turning his back on them and walking away; then he stopped, looked over his shoulder at them and said, "I agree. I shall call upon my men."

Elves came from the fortress approaching the Centaurs, neither comfortable with this plan. These awkward moments would later be remembered with dislike, but today, this was a necessary union of the two cultures, working together for a common cause. As the Centaurs carried their cargo, King Ananon again reflected upon his boyhood days. Today would fulfill his dreams to take back what was stolen from them so many years ago.

--------------------<>--------------------

The Centaurs carrying the Grass Elves moved quietly, but quickly over the terrain under the cover of darkness. As they arrived at the base of the castle, King Ananon, Solomon and Demetrius looked up at what faced them, the moat around the castle and the sharp steep wall of the mountain. On top of the mountain stood the dark rugged castle.

"Our men are quite adept at climbing," said

Ananon. "They have Elvin rope which will allow them to scale the steep sides and into the castle from behind and to the side. Farewell, my new friends. We WILL meet again! Good hunting!"

Ananon slid off of the back of Demetrius, the other Elves following his lead. At once the Tree Elves began their tedious job of using rope and hook to climb. The Centaurs waited for the Elves to get into position before they attacked, with only the dark to shield them from the enemy.

Pen It! Publications, LLC

Chapter 21

The children and Toron had rested just long enough to collect themselves. But it was time to get on with their mission. The path into the castle looked extremely rough and treacherous. As the small party of soldiers began to climb the rugged, steep face of the rocky fortress wall, they looked to the sky, still aware of the rushing water below them. It would surely kill them if they were to fall into its grip. To be swept away would be the end of all things. The sky was as clear as they had ever seen and they began to focus on movement coming in and out of the clouds.

"Look! Dragons! What do we do, Toron?" asked Frederick.

"Keep climbing, children. Move quickly!"

"What? I can't hear you!" shouted Jemma. As she turned to look over her shoulder, she slipped, falling toward the raging river. Frederick reached in desperation to catch her but missed, causing him to lose his footing as well.

Screams and shrieks came firing into the air, but they did not all come just from the children. These shrieks were from the dragons flying toward them. One of the flying monsters swooped down and grabbed Jemma just saving her from the mouth of the watery grave; another grabbed Frederick; another Toron from off of the face of the cliff. They were being carried ever so gently upward to the peacefulness of the clouds. They stopped screaming, as they noticed the dragons did not hold them aggressively. Then the three looked up to see Jade coming.

"Look Jemm! It's Jade! He is alive and here!" shouted Frederick.

Surrounding Jade were the Dragons. As Jade came within shouting distance of the children, another very large dragon came from the entrance of the castle flying directly at Jade. When they collided, it was like the two dragons exploded in the air, throwing each of them backwards, rolling and flipping in separate directions.

The fight had begun. To the south, the children watched as the dragons circled above the Tree Elves. The Elves had made it across the desert but the Seltons were waiting for them. Catapults were loaded from the lookout towers of the castle and fired in the direction of the Elves attacking the castle.

Meanwhile, from the left flank came some strange equine beasts to join in the battle. On the right flank came a battalion of Grass Elves.

"Look, Toron, they came after all! The Centaurs came!" shouted Frederick.

Arrows were flying; fire was igniting through the air from the dragons targeting those on the top of the castle wall. Jade and Patarian, finally meeting for their destined battle, took to their own positions again and charged at each other. Their screams were piercing, fierce and angry.

While all of this was beginning, the dragons carrying the children and Toron flew higher to the safety of the sky. The dragons began to fly out over the ocean past the rocky cliffs along the back side of the castle. They could see the foamy white water as it crashed into the rocks. The threesome panicked, not knowing where these dragons were taking them. When they were high enough and far enough away, the lead dragon banked to the right bringing Toron about to the back edge of the castle, a position too high to be seen by the Seltons guard.

The large creatures carrying Jemma and Frederick and Toron became quiet and glided lower until skimming the back edge of the castle premises. There they dropped their cargo onto the top of the castle courtyard, well behind and out of sight of the battle action taking place outside the castle walls. No one would suspect their entrance from this point.

It had been a very long night, already full of treacherous adventures and near death experiences. As Toron and the children waited on the top of the castle's tower, they looked up to watch their new dragon friends fly over them and back to the front of the castle, taking out some of the guards along the way.

"Whoa! Did you see that?" whispered Frederick. "I am beginning to think with these fellas we have a chance to win here!"

The screams from the front of the castle and the people yelling were getting louder. "We must move, children," insisted Toron. "We need to make our way into the castle while their attention is to the front."

"Look! There is a door. It must lead into the castle dwelling. However, we do not know where to go from there. We do not know where to look for the key. For all we know, it is wrapped around Banion's neck! Talk about looking for a needle in a haystack!" whispered Jemma.

"Let's move," whispered Toron, waving his hand to the children in his direction.

Toron led Frederick and Jemma quietly across the top of the castle to the door. He drew his sword as he put his hand on the door latch, slowly pulling it open. The stairwell behind the door was dark, narrow, steep and uneven. They moved quietly but cautiously in and allowed the door to close behind them. An eerie silence surrounded them.

Their eyes adjusted to the darkness but they could see a light further down into the next level of the castle. They came to the bottom of the stairs, finding another door that opened into another guard level. They spotted another door, this one taking them inside the castle dwelling. This room was large, sparsely furnished, but empty of men or guards. It seemed odd to Toron that since the castle was being attacked that there would not be people around.

There was a sound from the other side of the room. They froze, Frederick and Jemma pasting themselves to the back of Toron. At this point they had nowhere to hide and they were vulnerable to their enemy. The sound revealed itself ...a small mouse that had run out to search for a morsel of food. As it ran across the floor, Toron watched to see where it went. A large unlit fireplace was fixed in the wall. The mouse ran to it and disappeared behind it.

Toron thought for a minute; maybe behind this was the way out. "Now if I were living here, I would want to have made an escape plan. Where would I put my way out? In the open? I think not...Let's see..." Toron walked over to the fireplace, children still attached to his back and he began to feel around the mantle and down its sides. Nothing seemed obvious; no levers or switches. So he stuck his head inside the fire pit area and looked at the flue handle.

"Hmmm, I wonder..." as he pulled the lever, the fireplace began to turn ever so slightly. It opened only enough to squeeze one human man through to another side. Through this entrance was a secret passage with stairs again winding their way downward. With sword still held in front of him, Toron led the way, beginning their descent to the dungeonous bowels of the castle.

Toron located a torch on the wall, lit it with his

flint and lifted it out of its seat. Looking down at the path before them, they could no longer hear the screams and fighting going on outside the walls of the castle. There was a deafening silence; its only interruption, an occasional dripping sound of water crashing onto the cold hard wet stone floor. The descent seemed more cave like than castle like. Perhaps the castle had been built on a cavernous structure. It was very old. It was a very long stairway with no stops or other directions to go except down. When they finally reached the bottom, it opened into an empty oval room.

"A dead end?" pondered Toron. "There has to be something somewhere. Look around, children, for another door, lever, or something."

"Did we step right into a trap?" asked Jemma. "Maybe this stairway was not a way for them to get away but a trap for people looking for them. Now what?"

Once again they began to feel the walls, moving their hands over the cold, uneven surfaces. Toron turned to talk with them, facing the entrance from which they had just come when he noticed a faint slit in the wall beside the stairs.

"There!" said Toron as he began feeling the slit around the broken stone. "Help me...PUSH!"

The children put both hands up on the stone wall and began to push with Toron against the rock. It budged!

"Harder! Push harder!" said Toron with hope in his voice again.

The stone door moved back and opened up into another area that had to be the deepest part of the castle, the pit of the castle. They all collapsed to the floor with exhaustion, breathing heavily from their efforts.

Then they heard a faint weak voice from somewhere. *"Hello, please help me."*

Pen It! Publications, LLC

Chapter 22

$\mathscr{J}$ade did not see the children. He was not hurt, but only stunned by the collision with Patarian. As Jade righted himself, he saw out of the corner of his eye the Centaurs coming.

"Yes!"

But in that same instant, he saw one of the Centaurs fighting a Selton below him. He looked so strong, so able. But then he saw another Selton coming up from behind the Great beast just as the Centaur was defeating the Selton in front of him. Jade swooped down from behind the attack, his fiery exhaust exploding onto the assailant, killing him and taking the Centaur by surprise. Jade swooped up again looking back at the Centaur who gave him a simple 'nod'.

The fighting continued, screeching metal against metal, dragon fire exploding like an igniting furnace. Screams were everywhere, as attacks were made and lives were taken. From the right flank rode the remaining Centaurs into the battle; Arrows flying, catapults slinging up to the castle and back into the mass from the castle walls. Some were aware enough to move in time; others were not.

Jade banked right, coming about to see where Patarian had gone. He was attacking another dragon, a smaller one that looked to have no experience in fighting. He was being badly beaten. Jade rushed to him, his strong wings slapping the air into submission. His airspeed gave him an advantage over Patarian and he slammed into him hard from the side of his neck. Jade could see blood spilling from the wound but Patarian would not stop. Jade ignited a fire ball into the wound with no mercy.

Patarian's ear-piercing call was loud and angry as he fell toward the earth. But he gathered himself and pulled up, gliding into the sky again. As he turned about he kept his eyes on Jade. The job of killing this dragon was not for his master any longer, but for his own revenge. Patarian was much bigger than Jade and he knew the land better. Jade could not let him force him out over the ocean water. He saw Patarian coming at him, fire blasting from his mouth and nostrils, screeching like nothing Jade had heard before. However, as Patarian approached Jade, he took a long deep breath to give the hottest blast he could. This one set Jade ablaze.

As he took one long breath, Jade flew fast directly at him, punching him again and again, tangling his talons into Patarian's. He continued to pound at his wound while Patarian struggled to unlock the talons. Blood was pouring from Patarian, but he found the strength to blow his deathly fire at Jade once again. While Patarian was weakening, so was Jade. The last blast of fire critically wounded Jade.

Pen It! Publications, LLC

Entangled with each other and unable to fly, they began to spin out of control, falling further to the ground as it was rising up to meet them. The ocean's edge was pulling them closer to its jagged, sharp teeth. Their screams filled the air. Below them were the sharp rocky protrusions that would surely finish them both off if they landed on them.

Pen It! Publications, LLC

Chapter 23

"*H*elp, Me...Please..." the small voice came again.

The three travelers stood up slowly, looking at each other, not exactly sure how to respond to this voice. Toron did not say a word, but put his finger to his lips signaling to the children to not make a sound and pushed them behind him once more. He still carried the sword and the light. The cave curved to the right, a horseshoe bend, from where the voice seemed to come. Toron peeked around the curve to see a man imprisoned behind bars. The man was small, painfully thin, dirty, scrappy hair and beard, and only a tattered long night shirt to cover him. He had obviously been there for quite some time. Reaching through the cold, metal bars the man reached for them, again calling out for help.

"Please...help me...please," he begged.

"Who are you? Who put you here?" asked Toron.

The man's breathing was labored, being weakened from lack of water and food.

"My name is Salazar. How did you get in here? What day is it? From where have you come? Please free me from this prison!" the man begged with the little strength he had.

"Why are you in prison?" asked Toron. The children appeared afraid and content to let Toron interrogate this person.

"Banion had me imprisoned because I failed to kill an elf that was disobedient to him," said the man.

"So you are a Selton?" asked Toron.

"I was...I guess you could say that I am...but I am only by name," said Salazar. "I have repented so many times while lying here alone in this place. I have seen the evil of this man and prayed for him to turn from his evil ways."

"I assure you, he has not," said Toron. "In fact, he has gone mad. The dwellers of this land are here to defeat him."

"What do you mean, 'dwellers'?" asked Salazar.

"The Elvin Nations, the Centaurs, and the Dragons have united to defeat Banion. After all of these years, the forces from around this land have become allies and they are taking back their homeland. As we speak, battles are going outside between the Seltons and these armies," Toron explained.

"I can help you!" exclaimed the man, with a little more excitement. "There, on the wall behind you, the key to unlock my cell," he said, anxious to be released. But it suddenly dawned upon him that if the fighting was going on outside how or why would these three be in here? Salazar stepped back, now a bit worried that he had said too much. Maybe they had been sent to kill him by Banion and if so they would know how disloyal he really was.

Not aware of Salazar's misgivings, Toron was skeptical of him. He had seen so much destruction from the Seltons. How could he trust this man who openly proclaimed to have served this evil? If Toron let Salazar out, he may try to run. If he is spotted maybe he would trade his freedom by turning against the three of them.

"When were you locked up?" asked Toron. "Were you here before Banion took over?"

Salazar dropped his hands off of the bars. If these three strangers were going to help him, he realized he was going to have to be honest about his past. "I came from a land that is far from here. My family and I were sent here by our Monarchy to explore this new land and its inhabitants."

"So you are a sailor by trade?" asked Jemma.

"More like a pirate, I bet!" interrupted Frederick.

"I was a fisherman by trade originally, but our family was poor and when the King asked for volunteers to do this exploration, I thought it might give us a new start. So, I went on this journey, only to be caught up in the lies and misdeeds of Banion. Because I was human, and there weren't many of us, Banion took a liking to me. He made me his captain. He ordered me to be in his service. When it came time to discipline others, he expected me to be cruel and brutal. He enslaved so many innocent people, took away the land and possessions that they treasured and separated families. I could not do it. For that I was thrown into prison. It has been a very long time since I have seen the light of day. Look at my wall," he said, revealing tally marks of days gone past...or what he thought were days.

Toron turned and looked at the opposite wall. Just as the man had said, the key was there. "How can we be sure that you will not run and turn us over to Banion?"

"All I have in the world is what is in this cell with me, the clothes on my back and a spoon that is nearly gone from me carving on the wall. My family is dead. I have nothing to gain by turning you into Banion. I seek refuge and freedom, neither of which I will receive from Banion. I ask you to trust me. I have nothing to give you but my word. I can help you get out of here. I know the tunnels out from this place," submitted Salazar clenching the metal bars. "Please..." he pleaded as he slid down to the floor begging.

Toron wrinkled his brow, as he pondered the decision. Without saying a word, he turned around and used his sword to lift the key ring off of the hook.

"I believe him," Jemma said in a faint voice.

"I think we should let him help us," said Frederick.

The young boy picked up the key and inserted it into the lock. As he began to turn the key, there was a loud noise from deep in the cave. Someone was coming and coming in a hurry. Frederick began to shake so violently that he could not make the lock work. He kept thinking, *hurry*, but his hands were not obeying. From around the corner they spotted the source of the noise.

"The Warlock King!" Salazar exclaimed. "Doomed! We are doomed!"

Morpheus didn't stop, as he rounded the corner of the room. He laid his eyes upon Frederick first and began to chant a spell. Toron lifted his sword jumping in front of Frederick, prepared to do battle. The sword, which had been Elvin made, deflected the spell.

Another spell followed, only this one deflected from the sword back to its owner. As it struck the assaulting Morpheus, his breath seemed to be pulled out of him. He struggled to suck it back into his body. The Warlock King weakened.

Toron seized the opportunity to step up to him and pierce his sword into the evil creature's heart, the only way to kill a warlock. As Toron pushed the blade through, Morpheus fell to his knees, breathless, death coming for him quickly. Toron placed his foot on the creature's chest and heaved his sword back, reciting an Elvin magic spell causing the dying warlock to ignite. As flames roared, the Warlock King screamed, "NO! NO! NO!" until there was nothing else left of him but black ash.

"Hurry, Frederick! Get the gate unlocked! We have to move!" urged Toron. "Which way do we go Salazar?

"We have to find the key to the locket before we

leave here," said Frederick.

"Must leave...Must leave! Must get out!" mumbled Salazar with his new found freedom.

"Hold on there! We have to get the key first! You have to lead us down the cave. How much further until we get to the very end of it?" asked Frederick.

Toron had lost his patience and shoved Salazar up against the wall, clenching him around his neck. "YOU will show us the way and then you will lead us out of this forsaken place."

Reluctantly he went forward to lead the way, but he continued to mumble to himself. The smell of the burnt warlock and the damp dungeon was thick and sickening. Exhausted and weary, the small troop continued, picking up their pace for the sake of safety. They entered another room; this one appeared to be a dead end again.

"Search, children," Toron commanded. "It has to be here somewhere."

"Search where?" Jemma snapped back. "There isn't anything here but an empty room."

Toron continued to walk around the small space looking for a nick or cranny in the wall...someplace that would be a good spot to conceal something. "This is black magic. It is here somewhere, we just have to figure out the enchantment. Salazar, did you ever hear anything while you sat in your cell?"

"You know, I did hear something," Salazar answered.

The man thought for a minute, replaying in his mind the infrequent visits to this desolate place. "I remember Banion coming down here with that evil warlock. "The warlock would say something like, '*By Dark of night and black of heart, reveal yourself*'. I couldn't see where the hidden place was, but they did not linger here," said Salazar.

But as Salazar spoke these words, the walls surrounding disappeared revealing behind them, not only an escape route, but a locked safe in the center of the floor beneath their feet. Hearts were racing. Had they finally found what they needed?

Once again their excitement was interrupted by the noise of someone coming.

"Quickly, get behind me, children!" warned Toron. "Salazar, protect the children!"

Just then another man entered, approaching with his sword drawn. Salazar recognized him at once. "Banion!"

Chapter 24

*T*oron prepared for the charge, pulling his sword up to protect the others. The two began to dual, circling each other, stabbing at each other.

As they fought, Banion in his playful, overly self-confident manner, began a conversation. "And who do I have the pleasure of killing today?" he laughed erratically.

Toron tried to focus on the dual, but he felt himself becoming angry, stabbing and missing, stabbing and missing. His small stature certainly left him at a disadvantage. Banion played with him, toyed with him, as the brave Elf fought for not just his life but for his young companions' lives too.

"And who are these little people...the children? I haven't seen people like this for ..." he stabbed at Toron... "for a very long time. Might they be from my old world? I see..." he stabbed again and nicked Toron on the shoulder... "My dragon is fighting another dragon; one that my wizard knew as a human in Duradane."

Toron flinched at the swipe from Banion's blade. "Who was this human you speak of, Banion?" asked Toron, trying to concentrate on the sword fight and trying not be stabbed again. Toron charged at Banion with all his might, again missing. Banion's blade caught Toron's sword and slung it out of his hand. Banion kicked the Elf to the floor and held his sword to his chest. He had his foot on him, holding him down.

"The human...It was King Theyman," Banion said, as he slowly pushed his blade into the Elf's chest and through his heart.

The children heard Toron's sword hit the stone floor and his last gasp for air, his aching wince, as life fought to escape his body.

"Dead! NO! NO!" shouted Jemma and Frederick, mortified at what had just happened.

Banion was laughing hysterically. He was insane and quite out of control. "Who is next? Come on, don't be shy..." Banion said still laughing.

It was then that Salazar showed his allegiance. As he pushed the children to the ground, he dove to the floor grabbing Toron's sword and flipped over on to his back prepared to fight. Banion charged him. Salazar, weakened man that he was, found the strength to slap Banion's sword from his grip and stab Toron's blade into Banion's body. There was the gasp of air as life immediately left his body, Banion falling to the ground, now motionless. Silence filled the air. Jemma and Frederick stood in shock looking at their friend and leader appearing lifeless. Their fear and terror was tangible.

The children ran to Toron's body, screaming for him to wake up. Life was rushing from him. As he reached up to the children's faces with his hands, he mumbled to them, "You have done well, my faithful soldiers. Finish the task. Remember me and......" as his was voice fading, his hands dropped to the floor, grasping one last time for air. Death took him. They hovered over his body crying. He had been a man of great strength, honor, and courage, willing to lay down his life for good, for his country, for them.

"Children," interrupted Salazar, who had gone to Banion to look at him, making sure he was indeed dead, said, "I am sorry for the loss of your friend, but did you say you were looking for a key? Look, around his neck," Salazar said, drawing Jemma and Frederick's attention from Toron. "It's a key. Might this be the key for which you seek?" Salazar looked around the room for anything that would require a key. Banion had obviously come to the dungeon to get something and this key was not a prison door key. "What do you think? I am curious about what has happened outside the castle?"

Frederick, still hovering over Toron, wiped his eyes and nose on his sleeve, trying to clear the tears, so that he could see what this man was talking about. He laid Toron's hand on his chest and bent over to kiss his head, then got up to go see what Salazar had found.

Still in shock and not focused on the key, Frederick began to mumble, answering Salazar's most immediate question about the happenings outside the castle.

"When we entered the castle, there were forces

attacking from the south, east and west; the dragons, Centaurs, and different Elvin clans had come together and were taking on Banion and his evil Seltons," Frederick explained.

Just then, Jemma remembered that Jade was out there fighting too. "Frederick, we have to get that key and get back out to Jade! What if he is in trouble…or…," she couldn't bear to say what she was thinking…"dead."

Salazar continued to scan the room for anything that might need a key. They had discovered this locked box before Toron was attacked, but the key didn't look like it would fit that. Then he remembered, "There," he exclaimed. "There is a lock on the floor inside my cell. I wondered what that was. Here, try the key in it."

Frederick snatched the key from Salazar's hand and scurried into the cell. He fell to his knees and inserted the key into the lock, turned it and heard the click, click, click of the latch releasing. Frederick lifted the door back to reveal a deep, dark hole. "I can't see! It's too dark!" said Frederick.

Jemma jumped up from Toron's body and ran to join Frederick in the cell. She too fell on her knees to look into the hole. Without hesitation, she reached in, as far as her arm would allow, and with her fingertips felt the cold jagged edge of metal. "I got it!" she exclaimed, pulling the key from its hiding place.

Running to show Salazar their prize, the three new companions began to hear a low hum. Frederick and Jemma had heard this before, but in a different place. The hum became increasingly louder, stopping the children in their tracks. In front of them was a red glow emerging. The glow of the light grew and morphed into a large creature, recognizable only to Salazar.

"Froc!" he murmured.

"Who comes to steal from the Master?" Froc said, in a slow deep voice.

"Your Master is dead!" said Salazar.

"Silence! You and your young friends are about to die. This will be my Kingdom!" announced Froc.

As the evil wizard said this, he pulled his staff out from under his cloak to cast the death curse upon the helpless victims. Once again, Salazar pulled the children to him and pushed them behind him.

Suddenly, another hum erupted in the dungeon. Another glow of light revealed itself. It was the light that Jemma and Frederick had seen before; it was the White Wizard, Jarrod. His white light was so bright that even Froc had trouble seeing, squinting as though he were looking directly into the sun.

Jarrod appeared, directly facing Froc. As Froc began to cast the death curse, Jarrod uttered a counter curse. The wizards began to fight, good against evil, throwing curse after curse at each other. Frightened, the three humans crouched down to avoid the ricochet from the spells. As the fight continued, Jarrod seemed to grow larger, more powerful and dominated over Froc, forcing his power onto the evil Froc. When Froc could not hold Jarrod back any longer, he used the last of his own power to escape, disappearing into thin air.

Jarrod walked over to look. "COWARD!" the White Wizard shouted.

Jarrod turned to the children and said, "You must hurry! You are running out of time." The White Wizard began to fade. As his presence was diminishing he said faintly, "Find Jade; you must get to Jade; Find your King..."

"What did he say about the King?" asked Jemma. "Where did the other Wizard go? Sir, do you know how to get out of here?" Jemma asked Salazar. She was confused and didn't know what to do. The last time they were alone, was when they started this journey in the woods and found the Prince.

"I know the way. I know all the secret passageways in this dungeon," said Salazar. The children had a new sense of urgency as Salazar, having proved his loyalty led them through the passageway to the upper levels of the castle. They quickly approached the door opening onto the bridge that connected them to the outside world. A guard paced back and forth, protecting his post. Unsuspecting of their presence, the three-person army snuck up behind him.

They could now hear the fighting going on inside and outside the castle walls. They had become aware of other Elves in the castle who were dueling with the Selton guards. Many lay dead around them. As Salazar approached the gate guard, he ran with his blade drawn, ready to stab his victim. The guard was knocked down before he knew what hit him.

Salazar stood over the body waving the children onto the bridge. "Hurry," he whispered, in a demanding tone, then followed them to earn his freedom as well.

They all ran with purpose. They had their treasure and needed to get to Jade. As they shuffled to the other end of the bridge, Jemma and Frederick looked up to see three dragons swooping down upon them. The beasts' timing could not have been more perfect, once again rescuing the young children and their companion. The dragons picked them up as gently as they had the first time. Jemma spotted Jade. She yelled to the dragon carrying her, "Over there! Take us to Jade!"

Jade was lying on the ground. Fighting was still going on around them, but the battle between he and Patarian was finished. Patarian lay dead at the edge of the castle's moat. The dragons swooped in and landed, placing the three beside Jade, then took flight again to continue the victory over the Seltons. The battle was nearly finished and Banion was dead. The Warlock King was dead. The allied forces were taking over the castle.

Frederick knelt down on his knees next to Jade. "We're here, Jade! We got it! Oh, Jade, are you alright?" Frederick suddenly realized that their friend wasn't moving. "Jade! Jade!"

The dragon opened his eyes and looked at the children. "The key...you found it?"

"We did, Jade!" answered Jemma. "We have so much to tell you. Banion is dead and so is the Warlock King. This is our friend, Salazar. He helped us."

"Where..." Jade began, obviously weakened by his wounds. "Where is Toron?"

Reliving his death was too difficult. Neither child could speak.

Salazar stepped up to talk to Jade. "Mighty dragon, Jade, I am Salazar, a captain of the Seltons, imprisoned by Banion. Your friends have been so very brave. Toron and they rescued me from certain death. But I am sad to say that Toron paid the ultimate price. Toron and the children came to the dungeon and saved me. Banion had left me to rot in prison. In an effort to protect all of us, he fought Banion, but was overtaken. His name will be forever honored for helping to win this war."

Jade seemed to be fading quickly. But as he listened to what had happened, he shook his head in gratitude and relief. Many had died this day sacrificing their very lives to win back their homeland.

"Patarian...is he dead?" asked Jade.

All three humans looked around to see the other dragon lying lifeless. "Yes, he is dead," answered Frederick. "Jade, do you still have the locket? We need to try the key."

Again Jade nodded and then lifted his head to reveal the locket around his neck.

"Try it," Salazar encouraged.

Pen It! Publications, LLC

Frederick took the key from Jemma and inserted it into the locket. It fit perfectly. "Hang on Jade! We are almost home," exclaimed Jemma.

As Frederick inserted the key, the wind began to pick up and swirl around them. Lifting them into the center of a growing tornado, they felt themselves moving up high into the air and above the clouds, along with Jade. The roaring of its power spoke to them; its unintelligible sounds and power was in control of their fate. The children tried to look down, but they were moving so fast and the twister was carrying them too fast. They held their breath and held onto each other afraid of the possible outcome.

Frederick grabbed the key out of the lock. "What if we are too late? What if we cannot get back?" Frederick yelled above the noise of the twister.

All at once, Jemma and Frederick felt themselves falling. They grabbed hold of their beastly friend and landed with a thump on the hard dark space. That sudden piercing silence, that was all too familiar, surrounded them again.

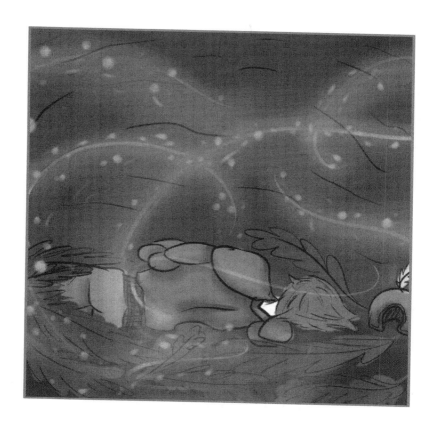

Pen It! Publications, LLC

Chapter 25

*T*he cave in Duradane remained cold and dark. There were no sounds; it felt lifeless and without hope. Time seemed to pass without notice. However, within this dwelling, lying under the blanket of old leaves, was Darian, who had been left to safely wait for this world's redemption. How much time had actually passed? There was no way to know and no one to keep the minutes, hours and days. Time passed in its own lonely way...waiting for what it did not know. However, Prince Darian had been put under a spell, one from the dragon which, with a single tear, bore healing and memory, sadness and compassion.

As Prince Darian slept, he dreamt of when he was a little boy. He saw himself in the castle with his father, enjoying a feast and planning a hunting trip. Slipping in and out of consciousness, he dreamt of meeting two runaway children.

"I need to help you..." he murmured.

Then his dreams took him to the festival. Looking through the crowd, he saw his father.

"My King!" he tried to say, but it was as though the Prince could not be seen or heard. He watched, from across the party of people, his father, the King, bid his farewell and begin to leave the celebration for the castle. Prince Darian followed...and he watched. As he watched, he could feel everything the King was experiencing revealing what really happened to his Father.

There was something eerie about this evening, as the King walked. Why it should seem so different than other times past, the King did not know. The only sounds he heard now were the sounds of the soles of his boots tapping the rocked path, as he walked. This eeriness began to make the King uneasy. He began to walk faster, unaware of his change in pace. He suddenly became afraid. He walked even faster. Beads of sweat were breaking out onto his brow. Had he had too much wine this evening?

He walked faster then stopped, considering his surroundings, and looked around, seeing nothing in the vastness of the dark. He began to walk...faster, faster. He was becoming breathless, his chest heaving, partly from fear and partly from the quick long strides of his pace.

"What is wrong with me?" he thought to himself, unaware of having ever known panic like this before... "And why am I so uneasy?" His thoughts were racing.

Fear now dominated him...sweating, thinking only of his destination; but again, he suddenly stopped. The sound of his heart beating was so loud, he knew that it would be heard by anyone listening, giving his *presence away.*

The path lights were gone. When had they been blown out? Had the wind been blowing? Funny that he would not have noticed the wind. He looked to the side of the path and there on the ground laid his wife's maiden and the two knights who had been accompanying her. Thoughts of panic began to run through him. Where was Queen Maritta? Was she safe? Had someone taken her? Then suddenly, before him he beheld an emerging red glow, glowing red as fire.

His amazement would not let him continue. But fear had turned into worried bravery for his beloved wife. He could not move forward...the light grew larger. Trembling, he began to back away, only to stop, as the light seemed to embrace him.

From this small red glow emerged a great wizard. His face was covered with the hood of a black tunic, blood red dragons embroidered on the front. This creature was tall; tall like the great giants of old of whom King Thaymen had heard told. The King was mesmerized, frozen in the unexplained occurrences of what was happening. With a great "thud", this wizard pulled from within his cloak a staff, also black with some kind of unrecognizable creature on the top of the rod. With both hands around it, he hit one end on the ground while holding it vertically directly in front of him. The earth seemed to shake and rumble as though an earthquake was occurring.

"I am the Black Wizard, Froc. I have been sent

to place you in captivity. Your Kingdom is to be overthrown by those known as the Seltons, whom I obey and serve. My reward is to be ruler of this kingdom."

The King could not believe his eyes. How could this be?

"Where did you come from, Froc? Why would you do this?" the king pleading for understanding.

Why had someone not come to his aid? Had no one heard this great creature, this monster? His voice was so loud. He was sure his people would have heard him in the valley.

But no answers were given. Froc began to laugh...echoing louder and louder. And with a wave of his staff, Froc cast a spell upon the King, incarcerating him within the confines of a large golden sphere. With another wave of his staff Froc sent this sphere into an unknown cavernous abyss, deep within the misty darkened woods, thought never to return again.

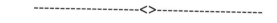

Darian awoke at the sound of someone screaming; it was his own scream and the realization of what had happened was not a dream. The evil Froc had attacked his mother and his father. "I must find him," he murmured to himself.

As he woke up, becoming more familiar with his surroundings, he tried to remember how he had gotten there. He sat up, looked around, and stretched his arms and legs. They seemed to work okay. He stretched his neck from side to side, stiff but working. He twisted his waist feeling the relief from the stiffness after laying in one position for who knows how long. He wiggled his toes, circled his ankles, first one way and then the other. All seemed to work.

"Dare I try to stand up? Are you working legs?" He turned to one side to hoist himself up first to his knees and then to his feet. Pushing himself up to a standing position, he felt the strength explode in his body. He stretched reaching to the ceiling of the cave while making the groaning kind of sound that feels so good when you first awake. Something had awakened him...or was it just his own scream?

"Hello!" he called out, hearing only the echo of his own voice calling back to him. "Hello!" Again his own voice answered mockingly back.

Darian sat back down in the stillness of the secluded cave unsure what to do. A breeze swept over his face.

"Odd," he thought. "Where would that have come from? Maybe there is an opening for me to get out."

This gentle breeze grew and began to swirl around the room. The harder it swirled the more violent it became, pushing the prince back. The tornado-like spinning grabbed the floor into its possession, Prince Darian with it, and scattered the dust, leaves and debris around. The floor began to shake.

"CRACK!"

A flash of light penetrated the darkness; then another "CRACK!" A thunderous sound was like none that Darian had ever heard.

All at once the wind stopped, dropping him to the floor. But now he wasn't alone. Beside Darian lay Frederick and Jemma along with a monstrous beast.

"I remember you!" Darian said. "You were the children I was going to help in the forest. What happened? Where have you been and why was I here by myself? Is this a dragon you have with you? Are you both okay?"

Before the children could answer, Jade began to wake up. Weakened, he managed to also ask if the children were okay. "Were we successful? Why am I still a dragon?"

Jemma and Frederick sat up from their fall and repositioned themselves next to Jade. The Prince sitting next to them, looked at all of them intently.

"Why hasn't it worked?" Jemma said bewildered. "Why hasn't he turned back? Nothing has changed."

"Wait, Jemma, the key; the key to the locket; we could..." started Frederick.

"What is happening?" persisted Prince Darian, still confused.

"We can answer all of your questions shortly. Do you see the locket around the dragon's neck? Here,"

Frederick said, "take this key and unlock the locket, Prince Darian."

"What key? Where did the locket come from and how did it get around his neck?" asked the Prince.

Jemma said, "After you were attacked in the woods, we thought you were going to die. We drug you into this cave and found this egg and…" continued Jemma.

"Egg!" exclaimed Darian. "The egg was the King! I just had a dream about it! How do we turn him back?"

"What? The KING? We don't know, Prince, but when we inserted the key it sent us home," said Jemma. "Maybe if you unlock it, he would turn him back. Hurry, he is dying."

Darian looked at the key that Frederick was holding, his eyes darting to the locket wrapped around Jade's neck. Darian looked at Frederick again and grabbed the key from him. As he reached for the locket, the large creature opened his eyes ever so slightly. Quiet tears began to run down the sides of Jade's face but he was too weak to speak more than a whisper. "Please…do it…" he begged in the Prince's ear.

Darian looked deeply into the eyes of the dragon, the King, his father, who lay wantonly. With one quick grab, he lifted the locket with one hand and inserted the key into its home with the other hand. As the key had fit so perfectly into the locket before, this time the locket began to glow. Darian turned the key with ease…click, click. A hum began to grow and the glow from the locket grew to encompass the dragon. The hum grew to a roar, the light blindingly bright. The cave walls began to crack, the barred entrance exploding open to reveal the way out.

As the hum and the light faded, laying on the ground was not the great dragon, Jade, but a man, a man who was near death. Prince Darian came closer to him and began to weep. The recognition of the man took his breath.

"My Father! Oh, my Father! It was you! My dream was true!" exclaimed the son. Darian continued weeping trying to speak through his sobs. "All of this time we thought you were dead. I have longed to see you. Please, Father, come back to us! Tell us what to do to heal you....I love you."

"The children...are they safe?" asked the King.

"We are here, Your Highness. We have been on a wonderful adventure together. You defeated the evil Lord Banion and his dragon, Patarius. Do you remember?" Frederick asked.

A small smile swept across King Theyman's face. "Sounds like a good story..." he said barely audible.

"You are a hero," said Jemma, unable to fight back the tears.

"The king was so weak. He knew his time to die was drawing near. He called to his son, "My son, it is time to pass on to you the throne of our forefathers. You have been trained well in the ways of leadership and goodness." The King began to drift into sleep, his eyes closing in spite of his effort to keep them open.

"As I close my eyes, I see a beautiful land of prosperous, happy people rising from the depths of despair, from a dark abyss, to a beautiful sunrise on the horizon. For all of this, I lay my life down. I see a young, loving King reining with the glory of his Lord to lead his way. It is you, my son that I see. To lay down my life for the good of our people, for our country...never have I felt so noble."

The King's breathing was becoming more and more labored. "Go...Go and live...live for me...rebuild what was broken."

Weakening, King Theyman, in and out of consciousness remembered those images of who he was, a gracious King, with his son playing with him in the courtyard...a game of hide and seek, hearing a small child's voice, 'ready or not!'". He heard the laughter of the child's mother, his beloved wife. These were such precious times. Suddenly the peace of this moment was interrupted by a sudden sharpness of pain; he opened his eyes again. There before him was his son, cradling him, tears falling onto the father he loved so deeply.

King Theyman reached up to touch his son's face and began to speak, his breath uneven and strained. "My son, you are now King." He struggled to continue. "Evil has been defeated...and from this wasteland will arise our beautiful land. While evil corrupted me and turned me into this monster, I am restored to life...my fathers' await my coming,"

The King gasped for air, Darian continued to cry and mourn his father. "We will meet again, my son, in eternity...together forever...a place fairer, brighter, where there will be no darkness...do you see the light, my son? There, you see...Father..."

The King grimaced in pain. Theyman opened his eyes to look into his son's eyes one last time. "Beautiful eyes...beautiful son...My King." And he closed his eyes in peace. His hands dropped to his side and his spirit left him.

Darian wept bitterly, as he gathered him up into his arms and cradled his father, a man he loved, a man who had given everything of himself for others. "Oh, my Father, your tears healed me, yet my tears fall in vain. Don't leave me!"

Jemma and Frederick cried with him, feeling his sorrow and pain. This man whom they had only known from afar as King, had been their friend, their protector, their ally, as they journeyed together to save the Kingdom of Duradane. This day...a day that should have been celebrated, was indeed bittersweet. As the three mourners sat hunched over their departed sovereign, they heard a voice behind them.

"Your Highness! Are you all right? Come and see! You must see what has happened!" insisted the voice of a fellow knight.

As the three persons reluctantly raised themselves to see what lay outside, they each leaned down to kiss the King goodbye. Darian took the necklace from his father's neck. "I will tell your story throughout future generations, Father. Your name and sacrifice will forever be remembered."

Rising, the three walked together to the opening of their newly opened prison, this doorway to the new world, no longer held hostage by the evil ways of Banion, the Warlock King and the Evil Wizard. Before them their land had been reborn. They looked out of the cave onto a land of beauty, a Garden of Eden, a new beginning...a new Duradane.

Author C. M. Bolte grew up in a small agricultural community in Indiana during the 1960s. Her parents had a deep love for reading; however, Cindy somehow struggled to share that love as a child. While in elementary school, reading was always difficult and writing never seemed to be on the radar. It wasn't until college, through a dear friend's help and encouragement, that the world of reading was opened up, allowing her to travel to places beyond her dreams.

In high school she became interested in genealogy, traveling with a relative to discover hidden secrets about their ancestors. She began reading memoirs that her grandmother had written and became interested in writing herself. Her interest in writing and reading grew even more after college while working in an elementary school where she had opportunities to help children to improve their reading skills through small reading groups and a specialized reading program designed to help students and adults (SRA). It was during this time that Cindy began to write poetry, eventually being a finalist in the Pen It Magazine Poetry contest, as well as dabble in writing some Reader's Theater scripts for the elementary school in which she worked.

Riddles for the Kingdom has been eight years in the

making. It began as a story writing journey with her three children, all contributing something to its creation and to whom she dedicates this book.

Cindy is a graduate of Ball State University with a degree in Social Work. She lives with her husband and children in Columbus, Indiana and is a Teaching Assistant for one of the local High Schools. In her spare time, she enjoys cooking, fishing, and quiet time by the lake, and spending time with family. Cindy's deep faith in God and family has truly motivated her to help others. May this book touch the hearts of those who read it and help you reach those places beyond your dreams.

122

Made in the USA
Lexington, KY
04 April 2017